CHARLIE BUMPERS vs.

THE
PERFECT LITTLE
TURKEY

CHARLIE BUMPERS vs.

THE PERFECT LITTLE TURKEY

Bill Harley
Illustrated by Adam Gustavson

Ω
PEACHTREE
PUBLISHERS

Published by
PEACHTREE PUBLISHERS
1700 Chattahoochee Avenue
Atlanta, Georgia 30318-2112
www.peachtree-online.com

PJF
HARLEY
BILL

First trade paperback edition published in 2016

Edited by Vicky Holifield
Design by Nicola Simmonds Carmack
Composition by Melanie McMahon Ives
The illustrations were rendered in India ink and watercolor.

Printed in July 2016 in the United States of America by RR Donnelly & Sons
in Harrisonburg, VA
10 9 8 7 6 5 4 3 2 1 (hardcover)
10 9 8 7 6 5 4 3 2 1 (trade paperback)

Library of Congress Cataloging-in-Publication Data
Harley, Bill, 1954-
  Charlie Bumpers vs. the Perfect Little Turkey / by Bill Harley ; illustrated by Adam Gustavson.
    pages cm
    978-1-56145-835-6 (hardcover)
    978-1-56145-963-6 (trade paperback)
  Summary: "It's Thanksgiving in the Bumpers household and Charlie has to be the perfect host to his annoying little cousin, Chip"— Provided by publisher.
  [1. Thanksgiving Day—Fiction. 2. Family life—Fiction. 3. Cousins—Fiction. 4. Humorous stories.] I. Gustavson, Adam, illustrator. II. Title. III. Title: Charlie Bumpers versus the Perfect Little Turkey.
  PZ7.H22655Cf 2015

[Fic]—dc23   2015006621

This book is dedicated with gratitude to
Roberta and Willard Block
for their support and love over the years.
And for all the Thanksgiving dinners, too.

Special thanks to Jane Murphy and Kassie Randall
for their careful reading; David McConville
for discussions about turkey psychology;
Althea Gunning, Gary Gunning, Richard Gunning,
Vince Fleming, and Dennis Langley
for their input on Jamaican speech; and as always—
to Vicky Holifield for her fine editing
and Debbie Block for everything else.

Contents

1

Holy Moly

Bumpers passes the ball up the field! The wing passes it back to Bumpers! He takes the ball on the run and puts it between the defender's legs. Unbelievable! The defender loses his shorts!

Bumpers on the left. He sees an open man! A perfect looping pass! This kid is only in fourth grade, but no one can stop him!

It comes back to Bumpers! The goalkeeper comes out! Bumpers lets go! A huge foot!

BAM!

Goal! Goal! Gooooooaaaaaal! The crowd goes wild! Bumpers pumps his fist. They win the championship! Bumpers kicks the ball into the crowd!

BAM!

He rips off his shirt and throws it to the fans!

I'm not supposed to kick the ball against the garage door because once I broke one of those little windows across the top. But that was a year ago, and I'm a lot better at kicking now. Anyway, Mom was out grocery shopping and Dad was in the basement. Charlie Bumpers, ace striker, was safe.

I danced around and pumped my arms in the air, celebrating my victory.

Matt, my older brother, stuck his head out the back door. "Hey, genius!" he called. "You're not supposed to kick the ball against the garage."

"I'm not hurting anything," I said.

"You're going to get caught," he warned, "and I won't defend you."

"Thanks!" I yelled.

"What a turkey," he said, then went back inside.

"You're the turkey!" I yelled, just as my little sister Mabel stepped out onto the back porch. My dad calls her "Squirt," but I call her "the Squid." It's funnier.

"I'm not a turkey," she said. "And your shirt is on the roof."

I looked up, and there it was, hanging off the edge. I kicked the ball again.

BAM!

"I'm telling!" the Squid yelled.

Just then, Mom pulled in the driveway.

I started dribbling the soccer ball between my feet, like I hadn't done anything wrong.

"Charlie's kicking the ball against the door!" the Squid shouted as Mom turned off the motor. "And he's not wearing his shirt!"

What a traitor!

I grabbed the rake leaning by the garage door and snagged my shirt off the roof.

I put it on just as Mom got out of the car. "Your

dad and I told you not to kick the ball at the garage door," she said, frowning. "Please come help me with the groceries."

I gave the Squid a dirty look and kicked the ball against the garage one more time, but not as hard.

BAM!

"Charlie!" Mom shouted.

"He's kicking the *b-a-l-l*," my sister said.

The Squid had just learned to read, and she'd started spelling everything out like she was a human dictionary.

I lifted two of the heavy grocery bags out of the trunk and followed Mom up the back steps into the kitchen. She'd bought tons of food for Thanksgiving dinner.

There are lots of good things about Thanksgiving. Like no school. And my grandparents coming. And the stuffing my mom makes. And the rolls my grandmother always brings, which are the absolute best food on the planet. But this year was going to be even better because on Thanksgiving evening a Buck Meson special was showing on TV.

Buck Meson, Detective from Andromeda, is my absolute favorite superhero. He has his own TV show and he's got this electron stare that paralyzes bad guys in their place so they can't move.

I know he's not real, but he should be. That would mean electron stares are real, and I would have many uses for them. Like paralyzing brothers and sisters.

When Mom and I had finished unloading the groceries from the car, our dog Ginger sniffed at the bags we'd left on the floor, looking for something to eat. Dad came up from the basement. "Wow," he said, looking at all the overflowing bags. "Is there anything left at the supermarket?"

"I asked Mrs. Walcott if she wanted to come for Thanksgiving," Mom said, ignoring my dad's joke. "She's going to be alone, so I thought it would be nice."

My mom's a visiting nurse. She goes to people's homes if they can't get to the doctor's office. Mrs. Walcott has been one of her patients a long time, and I've even visited her house with my mom.

"Uh-oh," Dad said.

"What?" Mom asked.

"Well, I thought we were going to invite the Gritzbachs this year."

Oh no, I thought. *Not the Gritzbachs!* Mr. and Mrs. Gritzbach are our neighbors. Mr. Gritzbach's kind of grumpy and can't stand our dog Ginger.

"I know," Mom said, "but I decided to ask Mrs. Walcott instead. She'll be completely alone if we don't have her over here."

"Hmmm." Dad looked worried. "I just invited the Gritzbachs."

"Oh jeez, Jim! Why didn't you tell me?"

"I'm sorry. I ran into them while I was taking a walk this morning," Dad said. "Their son is spending the holiday with his wife's family, so they were going to be by themselves."

"What are we going to do?" Mom asked.

"Well, I don't think we can disinvite them," he said.

"Of course not. But where are we going to put everybody?" Mom grabbed the notepad and pencil we keep by the phone and sat down at the kitchen table.

She started making a list of everyone who was coming. There was our family, which included my mom and dad, me, Matt, and the Squid. Then there were my mom's parents, Pops and Gams.

"Don't forget the Gritzbachs," Dad said.

"And Mrs. Walcott," I added.

"And Sarah and Brandon and Chip," Mom said. "And Tilly."

Brandon and Sarah are my uncle and aunt. My cousin Chip is a year older than the Squid and two years younger than me, and he can be extremely annoying. Especially to me. Tilly's his new baby sister. Her real name is Matilda.

"Holy moly," Mom said. "That makes fourteen people."

"Wow," Dad said. "I hope you bought a really big turkey."

"Turkey begins with a *t*," the Squid explained to everyone.

Dad's phone rang. He pulled it out of his pocket and looked at the screen. "It's Ron," he said, walking out of the kitchen. "I'd better answer."

Ron's my dad's brother. Uncle Ron is the greatest.

"I wonder if we'll have enough food?" Mom said. "Maybe I should bake an extra pie." She scribbled some notes on the piece of paper while the Squid looked over her shoulder, trying to read the words.

"Mom, you don't write very neatly," the Squid observed.

Dad came back in the kitchen. "Guess what."

"What?" Mom asked.

"Ron broke up with his girlfriend, and he doesn't have anywhere to go for Thanksgiving." Dad paused.

"And?" Mom asked.

"I invited him here," Dad said with a guilty look on his face. "I had to."

"You think he wants to stay for the entire weekend?" she asked.

"Probably."

I love Uncle Ron, but I know he kind of drives Mom crazy. Once when he was here for a few days, I heard her tell my dad it was like having another kid in the house.

I didn't see anything wrong with having another kid in the house. If it was Uncle Ron.

Matt walked in. "What's going on?"

"We're having fifteen people for Thanksgiving," I said.

"No way!" Matt chortled. "That's a lot."

The Squid was still peering over Mom's shoulder, looking at the pad of paper. "I see the number 15," she said. "But what's that?" She pointed at something

9

on the paper. "Those squiggly letters right there. What do they say?"

Mom didn't answer. Matt looked over Mom's other shoulder and started to laugh.

"What's it say? What's it say?" the Squid squeaked, which she does when she gets excited.

Matt laughed. "It says, *'too many!'*"

"You got that right," Dad agreed.

Personally, I could think of one easy way to shorten the guest list: Have my cousin Chip stay home.

2
Fooled Again

Monday morning Mrs. Burke, my fourth grade teacher, handed out dictionaries so we could look up the definitions of the ten words she'd written on the board. They all had something to do with Thanksgiving. You know, words like "gratitude," "holiday," and "pilgrim." When we were finished, she said, "Now, for your homework assignment."

Somebody groaned.

"Yes," Mrs. Burke said, "it is time for all of the citizens in Mrs. Burke's Empire to do their duty cheerfully—or suffer the consequences."

Mrs. Burke talks like that all the time. It's her way of being funny.

Ha ha ha.

"Tonight," she went on, "you are to write your own definition for a particular word. The word is 'family.'"

"That's easy!" Sam Marchand blurted out.

POW!

Mrs. Burke snapped her exploding fingers. She has the loudest fingers on planet Earth. In Mrs. Burke's Empire, you're supposed to raise your hand before you speak.

"Sorry," Sam said.

"Okay then, Sam. What is a family?" she asked.

"Your mom and dad and sisters and brothers," Sam answered.

"What about grandparents?" Mrs. Burke asked.

"Well, yeah," Sam said. "Them, too."

Alex MacLeod had his hand raised. Mrs. Burke called on him.

"I don't have any brothers or sisters,"

Alex said. "So they're not in my family."

Josh Little put up his hand.

"Yes, Josh?" Mrs. Burke said.

"Aunts and uncles...and cousins."

"Oooh, oooh, oooh!" Samantha Grunsky, who sits behind me, waved her hand in the air like she was going to die if someone didn't call on her.

"Go ahead, Samantha," Mrs. Burke said. "Don't injure yourself."

Samantha cleared her throat in her bossy way. "In science, a family is a group of species that have something in common."

Samantha Grunsky always seems to know everything, and she's happy to remind you of that.

"Yes, Samantha, that is one definition of family."

"Wait!" Joey Alvarez called out.

Mrs. Burke held her fingers up to snap them, but Joey quickly raised his hand.

"Um…what if you've got pets?" he asked. "Aren't they in your family?"

Mrs. Burke smiled. "What do you think, class?"

Everyone started shouting out their opinions. Mrs. Burke let us argue for a while, then—POW!— she let go with another one of her deafening finger snaps.

Mrs. Burke called on Ellen Holmes next.

"A lot of kids live with just one parent," Ellen said. "And what about my friend who lives with one parent part of the time and the other parent the rest of the time?"

We all started arguing again. Finally Mrs. Burke called out, "That's enough, class. It sounds like there are a lot of different ways to describe a family. So tonight, I'd like you to come up with your own

14

definition. And I want you to be prepared to defend it in class tomorrow."

Mrs. Burke was sneaky. She'd fooled us again. She had gotten all of us interested in something, and now we had to write about it. What a horrible way to ruin a perfectly good learning experience.

3

Sometimes Grown-ups Are Completely Clueless

That night at dinner, each of us shared something that had happened that day. The Squid told how this girl in her class lost her tooth at home but it fell down the sink and her parents had to call the emergency plumber to save the tooth so she could put it under her pillow for the tooth fairy.

"That's a very expensive tooth," Dad observed.

"But Tanya only gets a dollar," the Squid said.

"A lot less than the emergency plumber," Dad said. "Well, Matt. Any big news to report?"

Matt told about this kid named Thad in his

English class who did a presentation about an author. Thad had dressed up like the author and pretended to be him. Then, in the middle of the presentation, he'd fallen over, twitched a few times, and pretended to die right on the classroom floor. "Mrs. Cummings ran over and asked him if he was okay," Matt said. "Thad sat up and told her that the author had died very young. It was brilliant!"

"I guess it's dangerous being an author," Dad said. "What about you, Charlie?"

"Today in class we had to look up definitions for a bunch of words. For homework, I have to write a definition of the word 'family.'"

"I assume you will describe your excellent older brother," Matt said.

"Ha ha ha," I said.

"I'm in your family," the Squid announced. "Family: *f-a-m…*" She looked over at Mom.

"The next letter is *i*," Mom prompted.

"That's what I was going to say," the Squid declared. "Family: *f-a-m-l-i-y.*"

"Close enough," Dad said.

"That reminds me," Mom said. "With so many people coming for Thanksgiving, our whole family is going to have to work together."

"Your mom's right," Dad added. "It's our job to be good hosts, so I expect everyone here to be helpful...and flexible."

"Of course," Matt said. "Flexible is my middle name."

"Your middle name is Arthur," the Squid said.

"Don't remind me," Matt said.

"And that brings me to the next point," Mom went on. "Aunt Sarah and Uncle Brandon and Tilly are going to stay at the Village Inn with Pops and Gams. But they'd like Chip to stay here."

She paused for a second and gave me a little smile.

I didn't like that little smile. It meant something.

"Chip's a very nice boy," Mom said. "And I think he's grown up a lot. Sarah says his teacher calls him 'the perfect little gentleman.'"

Perfect little turkey, I said to myself. Even though the adults don't seem to realize it, Chip *is* a turkey. His real name is Brandon, but that's also his dad's name, so everyone calls him "Chip." He's a giant pest. Last summer we spent three days with their family at a lake house, and every time I turned around he was right there, buzzing around like a little gnat, telling me what to do, and saying he could do it better. Even though he couldn't.

I had tried to be nice to him, but it's hard to be nice to someone who drives you bonkers. My mom told me he followed me around because he wanted to be just like me, and said I should be patient.

Sometimes grown-ups are completely clueless. Even mothers.

"So, he's going to have to sleep in someone's room," Mom said.

"He could sleep on the fold-out couch," I suggested. The family room was a long way from my room.

"I think Uncle Ron will be sleeping on the couch," Dad said.

Mom opened her mouth, but didn't say anything.

"Maybe he can stay with Mabel," I said, "since he's closest to her age."

"He can't," the Squid said. "My room's too small."

"What about Matt, then?" I asked. "He has the biggest room."

"I need all that room for my brain," Matt said. "I think he should stay with you, Charlie. He always follows you around anyway."

"There's no bed for him," I said.

"We'll bring in the inflatable mattress," Mom said. "Just like when Tommy sleeps over."

"But he's my friend!" I said. "Chip is different."

"Chip'll take up less space than Tommy," Matt said. "You'll barely notice he's there." He gave me his classic evil older brother grin. He knew Chip drove me crazy.

"He'll mess everything up!" I protested.

"He can't," Mabel said. "Your room's already a mess."

"Matt, Mabel, please stay out of this. Charlie, you can put away the things you're worried about," Mom said. "And you do need to clean up your room."

Boogers!

Now I not only had to let Chip sleep in my room, I had to clean it up for him!

"This isn't fair," I said.

As soon as I said it, I knew what was going to happen.

Matt and the Squid sang out together, "LIFE'S NOT FAIR!"

They thought they were being funny.

Ha ha ha.

"That's not funny," I said.

Matt grinned. "Oh, yes it is."

The Squid started to laugh.

"That's enough," Dad said. "If Charlie's going to let Chip stay in his room, we can at least be nice to him about it."

"But I didn't say he could stay in my room!"

"I think it's best for everyone if he stays there, Charlie," Mom said. "He likes being with you and—"

"It's not best for *me!*" I said.

"Calm down, Charlie," Dad said. "It's going to be okay. It's only for a couple of nights."

"It's going to be okay, Charlie," the Squid said, copying my dad. "That's spelled with an *o* and a *k*."

My whole family was teaming up against me. They were going to have a great Thanksgiving, and I was going to have to put up with that doofy little turkey! I folded my arms and stared down at the floor. Ginger came up and rested her chin on my lap.

"No pouting at the table," Matt said.

"Matt," Dad warned.

I glared at Matt. "When I write my definition for family, I'm just putting in Ginger and no one else. No brothers and sisters. And especially no cousins."

It was quiet at the table. I knew my parents didn't like what I'd said.

"I'm your sister," the Squid announced, "no matter what."

"How unfortunate," I muttered.

"That's enough, Charlie," Dad said.

"I'd like to be excused, please." I figured I'd better leave before I got really mad.

Dad nodded.

I got up and headed to my room.

"I'm still your sister!" the Squid shouted. "But I'm not putting your dish in the sink!"

4

My Dumb Family

I stomped up the stairs and down the hall to my room.

My *messy* room. The Squid was right. It was a disaster area. Again. There were clothes and toys on the floor and stuff piled on my chair and desk and an unfinished puzzle in the corner, lying next to a plate with the crust from a peanut butter and jelly sandwich on it. I had to climb over my backpack and schoolbooks to get to my bed.

And now I had to do my dumb homework, which included writing about my dumb family.

But first I had to clear off my desk. I had been

working on a model of Buck Meson's Transport Module, which takes him to distant planets (like Earth). It was amazingly cool and looked just like the one on the show. My dad had helped with the hard parts and it was almost done. It was the only thing in the room that wasn't messy. I picked it up and placed it carefully on my dresser.

I pushed everything on my desk to the side and pulled my notebook out of my backpack.

I did my math. Multiplication.

Then my social studies. Abraham Lincoln.

The only thing left was my definition of family. My family.

I stared at the paper and thought about Matt and the Squid and what had happened at dinner and having to clean up my room. And about Chip.

I didn't want to write anything.

"What are you doing?"

I looked around. The Squid was standing in my doorway.

"My homework," I said. "Go away."

"Are you still mad?"

"Yes, I'm still mad."

She came in anyway. She picked up the box that the Buck Meson Transport Module had come in. "Hey, look! It says *B-u-c-k,* Buck. I can read this! Buck Meson!"

"Out!" I shouted.

My mom opened the door wide and took the Squid by the shoulders. "Come on, Mabel. Leave Charlie alone."

"But I was just asking," she said. "I don't want him to be mad. And besides, now I can read 'Buck Meson.'"

"Good. Go put on your pajamas," Mom said.

"Grouch monster," the Squid said to me.

I made a face at her as she went out the door.

"Charlie," Mom said, "I'm sorry that you have to share your room, but even if you're mad, there's no reason to say what you said about Matt and Mabel."

"There's every reason!" I said. "They always gang up against me."

"You're just tired and upset right now. Put your homework in your pack and get ready for bed."

"I'm not done." I still had to write the dumb definition.

"You can have fifteen more minutes," she said as she left. "But then it's lights out."

Staring at the blank paper, I still couldn't think of anything to write. I glanced over at the Buck Meson Transport Module and thought about the TV special. I could hardly wait.

Matt stuck his head in the door. "Still pouting?" he asked.

"Get out!" I yelled.

"Touchy, touchy, touchy!" he said, disappearing down the hall.

Now I *really* didn't want to write the definition! And I especially didn't want to write about Matt and the Squid. So finally I scribbled down one sentence: "Family is a bunch of people you have to live with and share with even when you don't want to."

Then I stomped into the bathroom I have to

share with Matt and Mabel and slammed the door so no one would bug me.

"Whoever did that, no slamming!" my dad called up the stairs.

GRRRRR! I looked in the mirror and practiced the Buck Meson electron stare. You could always tell when he was going to give it, because his head made little circles like he was focusing. Then his eyes spun for just a second, and there was a flash of green before they shot out really bright beams of light.

If I had really done it while I was staring in the mirror, I probably would have fried my own brains.

When I had finished brushing my teeth, I turned the doorknob, but nothing happened. I tried again.

I heard a clunk on the other side of the door. It was the knob falling on the floor.

I turned the knob on my side again, and it came off in my hand. This wasn't the first time this stupid old door wouldn't open. Dad kept saying he was going to fix it, but never got around to it.

"Help!" I shouted, pounding on the door. "I'm stuck in the bathroom! Help!"

Nobody came.

"Help!" I yelled even louder.

Finally I heard someone coming down the hallway.

"Is that you, Charlie?" It was the Squid.

"Yes, it's me. The doorknob fell off again. Can you put it back on?"

"Okay," she said. But then I heard some more footsteps.

"What's going on?" Matt said.

"Charlie's in the bathroom," Mabel explained. "I'm looking for the doorknob."

"Here it is," he said. But he didn't open the door. "Hey, Charlie. Why'd you shut the door? You know you shouldn't close it all the way."

"I didn't want you guys to bug me. Please just open it."

"Are you still mad?" the Squid asked.

"Yes. Now please open the door."

"We'll open it when you're not mad." I could tell Matt was completely enjoying himself.

"No, Matt. We have to open it," the Squid said. "I don't want him to be mad forever."

I heard them messing around with the knob and then the door opened. They were both standing there grinning at me. I walked right past them to my room.

"You didn't even say thank you, and I was almost asleep when you yelled," the Squid said.

"Thanks for nothing," I growled.

"Grouch monster!" the Squid yelled.

"Bozo!" I yelled back.

I turned off my light and got into bed. I didn't even read, which I almost always do since it calms me down. I waited for my dad to come in and say good night so he could see how mad I was. But I guess I fell asleep before he got there.

Boogers.

5

A Special Assignment

"Who would like to read their definition of family?" Mrs. Burke asked the next day in class. A bunch of hands went up.

Not mine.

"Trevor," Mrs. Burke said. "Why don't you share yours with the class?"

Trevor David walked to the front of the room and started to read. "A family is my mom and dad and my brother Lewis and my Aunt Chloe and Uncle Drew and Aunt Melissa and my four grandparents—Grandma Celia, Granddad Herbert…" He just kept going. Forever. After a while, it got pretty funny, but Mrs. Burke let him read the whole thing.

Then other kids read their definitions.

The last line of Alexandra Burnett's definition was "Family is anyone you're related to."

"What does it mean to be related?" Mrs. Burke asked the class.

Samantha Grunsky's hand shot up like a rocket. Of course.

Mrs. Burke nodded at her.

"'Related' means you have some of their genes," Samantha said proudly.

"Blue jeans?" Sam Marchand asked.

Everyone cracked up.

Mrs. Burke told everyone to pipe down and called on Josh, who was patiently holding his arm in the air. Josh is always patient.

"It means some of your cells are the same," he explained.

"But what if you're adopted?" Ellen asked. "My friend Alicia has parents who adopted her."

"Like me," said Robby Rosen. "I'm adopted, too. But my mom and dad are still my family."

A lot of kids nodded. I already knew Robby was adopted because he told me in first grade.

I read my definition again. Now that I'd had time to cool down, it didn't look so good to me.

I glanced over at my friend Hector Adelia, who sits next to me. "Hector," I whispered. "Can I see yours?" He was usually a little shy, so I figured he wouldn't volunteer to read his aloud.

He handed it to me. Hector's handwriting is very neat, just like he is. *I think family is anyone you care about,* Hector had written. *Once you know someone really well, it begins to feel like they are family. So I think they are.*

"That's awesome," I said, handing the paper back. I slipped my definition under my notebook.

Crystal Medeiros, who doesn't talk a lot, was reading hers in a low voice. "My definition of family is the whole world. I think we're all related."

I wondered if this meant Samantha Grunsky was related to me. Matt and the Squid were bad enough—being related to Samantha would be a catastrophe.

Mrs. Burke stood up. "Okay, citizens. Please pass in your definitions. I'd like to look at them—we can talk about them more tomorrow."

Everybody but me passed their assignments to the front. "What are you waiting for, Charlie?" Mrs. Burke asked. "Pass yours up, too."

So I did.

What a bozo.

◆ ◆ ◆

The next morning in class, everyone was excited about getting out of school early.

I love half days.

The teachers realize they can't get everything done, so they don't even try. And since tomorrow was Thanksgiving vacation, we were about to have *two* extra days off.

During math, Mrs. Burke split us into pairs to

work on problems together, then sat at her desk to grade papers. Hector was my partner. The math problems were pretty easy. When we finished, I asked Hector if they had Thanksgiving in Chile, where he's from.

"No," he said. "In Chile right now, it's almost summer."

"Wow, that's weird," I said. I told him a little about Thanksgiving at our house.

"It sounds like it's mostly about food."

"Yeah, except I try not to eat too much in the morning," I said, "so I'm really hungry for the gigantic dinner."

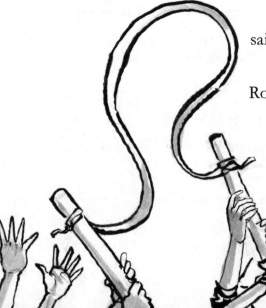

"Good idea," Hector said.

"And this year Uncle Ron is coming," I said. "I wish you could meet him. He's really fun. He usually brings something for us kids to do when he comes."

"Like what?" Hector asked.

"Well, once he brought this really stretchy surgical tubing that we turned into a giant slingshot that fired water balloons into the air. It was so cool. Three of them went over the roof of our house!"

Hector's eyes got big. "Really? Where did they land?"

"I don't know. We couldn't find them," I said. "And then one summer Uncle Ron brought these old tire inner tubes and we floated down the river really far and by accident we floated past where we were supposed to get out and then he dropped his cell phone in the water so we had to get a ride from someone we didn't know back to the car and were late for dinner and Mom was afraid we had all drowned."

"Really?" Hector's eyes got even bigger.

"Yeah, and Uncle Ron makes awesome stuff and he can fix almost anything."

POW! POW! POW! Mrs. Burke snapped her

fingers. "Hector and Charlie, if you're done with your math, please find something quiet to do so others can work."

When everyone had finished, Mrs. Burke handed back the definitions of "family."

Mine didn't come back. She still had one paper in her hand.

"I've made notes on your papers," Mrs. Burke said to the class. "I'd like you to rewrite them here in class and make the changes I suggested. If you want, you can take yours home and read it to your family at Thanksgiving. That's all the homework you have for the holiday."

Everyone clapped and cheered.

"So get to work!" she said.

She looked down at the paper she was holding. "Charlie, come up here for a minute, will you?"

Uh-oh. I did not like the sound of her voice.

When I reached her desk, she held up the paper. "Charlie, what's with this? Did you mean what you wrote here?"

"Kind of," I said.

"What do you mean 'kind of'?"

"Well, I know I was supposed to write about how great families are, but my brother and sister ganged up on me after dinner and they're always really bugging me and…"

She gave me one of her not-a-good-answer looks.

"And they locked me in the bathroom," I added.

Even that didn't seem to bother her. She just kept staring at me.

"And my cousin is coming for Thanksgiving and he follows me around and bugs me…and I have to let him sleep in my room."

"All this sounds tragic, Charlie," she said. "But I'm not going to accept this paper. I've got a special assignment for you."

"Okay," I said.

"You don't have to rewrite this now," she said.

"All right," I said.

"You don't have to write anything today."

I nodded. This was getting better and better!

"Instead, I want you to pay attention during the vacation to everything that happens at home. Then I want you to write a completely new definition. And I want you to explain why you wrote it. You can hand it in on Monday."

What? Was she kidding? What kind of special assignment was that? No one else had real homework over the long weekend but me!

"But…," I started.

"What?" she said.

"That's not fair," I said.

"Do you know what my mother always used to say?"

I already knew the answer. "Life's not fair," I mumbled.

She put her hand on my shoulder. "You can do a lot better than this, Charlie."

As I headed back to my desk, Samantha Grunsky looked up from her paper.

"Where's your definition?" she asked. "Didn't you hand one in?"

"I have a special assignment," I said.

"I bet you did yours wrong," she said. "What's your special assignment?"

I did not want to tell Samantha Grunsky about my special assignment.

"None of your beeswax," I said.

6

Already Driving Me Bonkers

When the Squid and I got home from school, we were surprised to find Mom already at the counter in the kitchen, surrounded by mixing bowls. "Charlie," she said, "please walk Ginger, she's going crazy."

I could tell Mom felt hassled, so I didn't complain. I took Ginger around the block. She peed and pooped and didn't even put one paw on Mr. Gritzbach's yard. That was good, because I didn't want him to be grumpier than usual when he came over on Thanksgiving.

When I got back, Mom was yelling up the stairs

for Matt to bring in some firewood. Then she asked Mabel to fold the napkins in the laundry basket.

Then she had orders for me.

"Charlie, you left some clothes on the floor of your room this morning," Mom said. "Please go straighten up. Everybody will be here in an hour or so."

Mom was acting like a marine sergeant. She always gets like this when relatives come. But you don't argue with a marine sergeant—especially when it's your mom.

I went up to my room and looked around. I had spent most of the afternoon the day before cleaning it up, and I thought it looked pretty good.

As long as you didn't look under the bed or in the closet.

There wasn't much room to walk, since Mom had also made me pump up the air mattress for Chip.

There was a pair of underwear and a T-shirt on the floor. I put them in the clothes hamper.

The transport module was on my desk. I had finished that the day before, too. It looked truly stupific. That's a word Tommy and I made up—it's a combination of "stupendous" and "terrific." The tiny Buck Meson was sitting in the cockpit like he was ready to take off. I still couldn't believe I'd put it together myself.

I shoved my backpack into my closet and smoothed out my bedspread.

When I came back downstairs, Mom had set out all kinds of ingredients. She looked a little like a mad scientist, mixing things up in so many different bowls.

A mad scientist marine sergeant.

The Squid was standing at the counter, reading aloud the labels on all the boxes.

"Charlie," Mom said, "I want to remind you again to please be a good host. Chip is only here for two nights, so I need you to be a good big cousin."

"Okay," I said.

"Thanks, sweetie. I really appreciate it." She gave me a big smile. "I'm so excited everyone's coming."

Okay—I guess even mad scientist marine sergeants can smile.

Just then, Matt opened the back door and marched in. "What's for dinner?" he asked.

"We're ordering pizzas," Mom said.

"Pizza begins with a *p*," the Squid announced.

"That letter makes the *puh* sound."

"Can we order them now?" Matt asked. "I'm starving."

"Too early," Mom said. "We have to wait for everyone to get here."

"I might starve," Matt said.

"You might." The smiling marine sergeant mad scientist didn't seem very concerned about her son starving.

"This says 'eggs.'" The Squid held up the egg carton.

"You're a genius, Mabel," Matt said.

"I know," the Squid said.

Mom kept giving us things to do, like fluffing up the pillows on the couch and vacuuming the rug. When Dad got home she had him rearrange the chairs in the family room. "And when you're done, please fix that bathroom door upstairs!" she called to him.

Before he could answer, we heard the front door open. "Helloooooooo!" a voice called out.

46

It was Aunt Sarah. Mom hurried toward the front door. The Squid was right behind her.

"Where's Charlie?" I heard someone yell.

It was Chip.

"Here we go," Matt said in a low voice.

When I went into the living room, Aunt Sarah was already there, holding Tilly in her arms. Pops and Gams were coming through the door. I didn't see Chip.

"Hi, Sarah! Hi, Tilly!" my mom said, her face breaking into a big grin.

"Hey, everybody," Sarah said. "Tilly, can you say hi to Aunt Gloria?"

Tilly took one look at us and buried her face in Aunt Sarah's shoulder. Aunt Sarah patted her back with a smile, and Mom laughed.

"Hello, folks," Pops said. "The army has arrived!"

"Hi, Dad!" Mom gave him and my grandmother big hugs. Then my dad came in and we all stood around for a few minutes, hugging each other and saying hello. Matt waved to everyone, then disappeared upstairs. Pops shook my hand really firmly, then laughed and pulled me into his belly.

As soon as Uncle Brandon said hello to everyone, he reached into his pocket and pulled out his phone. "Be back in a minute," he said, already punching in a number. "One phone call I've got to make."

"Charlie!" My grandmother put her hands on my shoulders and gave them a squeeze. "Just look how tall you're getting!"

"I grew, too!" the Squid said, pulling on Gams's arm. "Also, my brain grew and now I can read."

"Isn't that wonderful?" Gams exclaimed. "You're bright as a button! Just like Chip! He read to us all the way down here. My grandkids are absolutely amazing!"

"Hey, Charlie!" Chip called. I turned and saw him standing at the door to the family room, holding a couple of LEGO cars I had built. "I'm going to take these apart and build something better. Come on and watch me." Before I could protest, he ran back into the family room.

"Charlie," Mom said. "Why don't you show Chip where he's staying?"

I picked up his backpack. "Hey, Chip," I called. "Come on. Let's go."

I headed up to my room. When I was halfway down the hall, I heard footsteps pounding up the stairs.

"Charlie, wait!" Chip said. "I remember where your room is!" He pushed ahead of me and burst through the door first.

"We're sleeping in here together?" he said, looking down at the air mattress.

"Yeah," I said. "It's kind of crowded, but—"

"Awesome!" Chip fell down on the mattress. My mom had already put some sheets on it and it looked like a real bed.

"It's not very bouncy," he said. Then he climbed up on my bed and jumped up and down. "This is way better. Can I sleep here?" he said.

"Stop jumping. That's where I sleep," I said. "We blew up the mattress specially for you."

"Charlie, please? Just for tonight? Just one night?"

I wanted to say *No way, you little turkey. This is my bed!* But I didn't. "You'll like the mattress if you try it. I've slept on it before. It's really fun."

"Then why don't you sleep on it now?" he asked.

I thought for a second. It was just one night. I remembered what Mom had said about being a good host. "Okay," I said. "Just for tonight."

"Yippee!" Chip started jumping again. "Thanks, Charlie! This is a great bed!"

It *was* a great bed. *My* great bed. I turned and headed down the hall.

"Hey, Charlie!" Chip yelled. "Where are you going?"

I hurried downstairs and slipped through the kitchen, where the grown-ups were all talking and laughing. The Squid was there, too, and Ginger was barking because there were so many people.

I pulled my fleece off the hook and put it on, then went out to the garage for my soccer ball. I kicked it around the driveway, avoiding the garage door.

Chip bounded down the back steps. "Hey, great! Soccer!" he shouted. "I can kick it really hard."

"We're not supposed to—"

But before I could finish my warning, Chip booted the ball straight for the garage door.

BAM!

It came right back to him and he kicked it again.

"Chip—" I started again.

BAM!

This time it bounced toward me and I caught it. Just then the back door opened. "Charlie!" my dad said. "I've asked you a hundred times not to kick the ball at the garage door."

"I didn't!" I said. "I was trying to—"

"We're both playing, Uncle Jim," Chip interrupted. "We're seeing who can kick it harder."

"Okay, Chip, but not against the door."

"I didn't know," Chip said.

"Well, Charlie does," Dad said.

"Dad!" I yelled. It wasn't fair he was blaming me.

"Just kick it to each other," Dad said. "With two people you don't need a door. I'm going back inside. It's cold out here."

"Let's play in the driveway!" Chip said.

"I'm going inside, too," I said. Chip was even more annoying than I remembered.

"Okay," Chip said. He grabbed the ball and punted it toward the street, then ran up the back steps and into the house.

"Chip!" I called. But he was already gone. I ran after the ball. Uncle Brandon was standing at the end of the driveway, still on his phone. The ball had rolled right by him. I found it behind our neighbor's car. As I carried it back, Uncle Brandon waved to me and smiled. He had no idea what was happening.

Everybody was still in the kitchen, except for Uncle Brandon and Matt.

"Charlie!" the Squid said. "We're ordering pizza tonight. And I'm reading the menu." My sister was sitting at the table with Gams and Mom, holding the menu from the pizza shop.

"This says 'cheese'!" she said. "And this says 'peepers.'"

"Peppers," Gams corrected.

"Peppers! And I don't even know this word."

"That says anchovies," Gams said.

"What are those?"

"Little fish."

"Fish on a pizza?" The Squid shook her head. "Yuck. I don't need to know that word."

"Here," Chip said, snatching the menu out of the Squid's hands. "I can read the whole menu."

"Hey!" the Squid protested. "I was reading that!"

"I'm just looking at it for a minute," Chip said, "then I'll give it back."

"Okay, but only for ten seconds. One…two… three…"

"Mabel," Mom said. "Let your cousin read. I'm sure he'll give it back in just a few minutes." Then she went back to talking to Aunt Sarah.

While Chip read the whole menu out loud as fast as he could, I went over to Dad, who was leaning against the counter.

"Dad," I said. "I wasn't kicking the ball against the garage. It was Chip."

"Okay," he said, giving me a hug. "Just don't do it again."

"But I didn't do it!"

"I said it's okay, Charlie." Dad gave me another squeeze. But it was like he wasn't hearing me. There was too much going on.

Usually I pay attention when someone's ordering pizza. I like extra cheese on mine and nothing else. But instead I just wormed my way out of the kitchen and went upstairs. I walked down the hall to Matt's room. The door was closed, so I knocked.

No answer. I knocked harder.

"Nobody home!" Matt yelled.

"C'mon, Matt, it's me!"

"Seriously, there's nobody home!"

I could tell Matt was listening to music because he was talking so loud. I pushed the door open. My brother was lying on his bed with his headphones on, staring at the ceiling like a zombie. He looked at me, lifted one earpiece, and shouted, "Hey, illegal entry!"

"Please, can I come in for a second?"

"Permission granted," he said.

I closed the door behind me and sat on his chair. I didn't say anything. For a while, Matt just ignored me, but then he finally clicked off his music player and took off the headphones.

"What is it?" he asked. "Why are you bugging me?"

"Chip is already driving me bonkers," I said.

"Now you know what it's like to have a younger brother," he said with a satisfied smile.

"I'm nowhere near as bad as Chip! He won't sleep on the air mattress and he's taken over my bed. He's following me around everywhere, and Dad yelled at me for kicking the ball against the garage."

"You're not supposed to do that," Matt said.

"I didn't! Chip did it and Dad blamed me."

"I don't know what you're complaining about. Chip is a 'perfect little angel.' Just ask Mom and Gams and Aunt Sarah." He gave me his evil older brother grin.

"He is not! He's a perfect little *turkey!* What should I do?"

"Just try and ignore him," Matt said. "Like this." He put the headphones back on, hit Play, and stared at the ceiling again.

"Thanks a lot!" I yelled at him.

"You're welcome!" he yelled back.

7
The Loudest Whistle in the World

When Dad came back with the pizza, we all piled into the kitchen. By that time, Uncle Brandon had finished his phone call, and even Matt appeared out of nowhere.

"Look," Dad said, pointing at him. "He shows up when there's food."

"Hilarious, Dad," Matt said.

"Thank you." Dad grinned.

Mom set out plates and a big salad.

Dad opened all the pizza boxes and lined them up on the counter. "Double cheese for you, Charlie," he announced.

"That's my favorite kind, too!"
Chip yelped. "Let's have a contest and
see how much we can eat!" He took two
pieces and sat down at the kitchen table.

I couldn't help myself. I put three slices
on my plate and as soon as I got to my seat, I
started eating as fast as I could.

"Slow down, Charlie," Mom said. "Leave some
for everyone else."

No one told Chip to slow down. He was holding
one pizza piece in each hand and taking bites from
both.

"You've got a big appetite, little Chipster," Uncle
Brandon said.

Matt leaned over toward me. "So do you, little
Charlester," he teased. I saw that he had three pieces
on his plate, too.

We were almost through eating when we heard a
really loud whistle.

Uncle Ron!

Uncle Ron has the loudest whistle in the world, which he taught me to do last year. Without even thinking, I put my fingers in my mouth and blew really hard.

FWEEEEEEEEEEEET!

"Charlie!" Mom said.

"My goodness!" Gams put her hands over her ears.

By the time I got to the back door, Uncle Ron was standing there with a duffel bag over his shoulder. The Squid and Matt both bounded out of their seats. Dad broke into a grin. Ginger barked like crazy and jumped all over Uncle Ron. He knelt down and let her lick his face for a few seconds. "Okay, girl," he said. "Later you and I will do some wicked ball chasing, I promise."

Even though Uncle Ron is younger than my dad, he's way bigger. He loves to eat, and he looks like it.

"Hi, Uncle Ron!" I gave him a hug. When he squeezes you with his huge arms, you think your guts might come out somewhere, but it's still fun. His jacket smelled like wood chips and his old truck and the outdoors.

"Charrrrrlie!" he roared, putting me in a headlock and rubbing my scalp with his knuckles.

"Oowwwwwww!" I screamed. But I was also laughing.

He let me go, then slapped Matt a high five. "Yo, Matthew! A teenager! This means trouble." Matt gave Uncle Ron a goofy grin, which you hardly ever see him do anymore.

"Uncle Ron!" the Squid squealed. "I can read!"

"No, you can't!" he said.

"I can, too. I can read the pizza box! It says 'pizza'!"

"Omigosh, Mabel, you're a regular child prodigy!"

"I am?" the Squid said. I don't think she knew what

that meant, but I guess it sounded good to her.

"You are!" Uncle Ron nodded.

The Squid beamed. He picked her up and swung her around.

"I almost forgot!" said Uncle Ron, setting her down. "I've got something for you guys!" He put his duffel on the floor and unzipped it. He rummaged around for a second, then pulled out a huge plastic jar filled with candy.

"Swedish Fish!" he said, holding up the jar. "My favorites! But I decided to share them with you!"

There must have been three hundred pieces of candy in the jar. Stupific!

"Yippee!" the Squid sang. Uncle Ron handed her the jar, which was so big she could barely hold it.

I looked over at Mom.

She had a little smile on her face, but I knew she wasn't that happy with having so much candy in the house. Uncle Ron didn't seem to notice.

"Big brother!" Uncle Ron held his arms open for Dad. As they hugged each other, I heard Uncle Ron whisper in Dad's ear, "Thanks, bro. Thanks."

Dad was still grinning.

Then Uncle Ron went around and shook hands with everybody.

I noticed that Chip had opened the huge jar of Swedish Fish. I watched as he pulled out a big handful. "Hey," I said. "Uncle Ron didn't say we could open that yet."

"There's enough for everyone," Chip said and stuffed a bunch of them in his mouth. I was about to put the top back on the jar, but first I took a handful myself. I didn't even feel like eating any Swedish Fish. I was already full from the pizza. But I couldn't let Chip hog everything.

After a few minutes, Uncle Ron served himself some pizza and salad and sat down to eat. The grown-ups gathered around and started to talk. It seemed like a good time to leave. I knew things would get boring pretty fast—even Uncle Ron could be boring when he was talking to other grown-ups.

But just as I was leaving he called me over. "I've got something amazing to show you."

"What?" I asked. If Uncle Ron said something was amazing, it was *really truly* amazing.

"Plans for a rocket we can build. I've got everything we need in my truck. I just have to finish up the launcher tonight, and we'll build the rocket and shoot it off tomorrow."

"Cool! Can't we do it now?"

"Not now, you giant goofball. It's dark already. Tomorrow. That way we'll keep you morons out of the grown-ups' hair while they're trying to get dinner ready."

Mom smiled at that. Anything that would keep children occupied and stop them from driving her nuts was probably a good idea.

"All right," Dad said. "You kids run along so we can talk."

I could hardly wait for morning. I was hoping Uncle Ron and I could build the rocket by ourselves.

As we left the kitchen, Chip turned back. "What about me, Uncle Ron? Can I do the rocket, too?"

"Of course you can," Uncle Ron said. "The rocket launching is an equal opportunity experience."

Boogers.

Maybe we could send Chip up in the rocket.

8

Rocket Propulsion

The grown-ups came into the family room around nine. Dad turned off the TV. "Big day tomorrow," he said.

"This is vacation, Dad," I said. "Can't I stay up later?"

"Maybe a little while, but Aunt Sarah and Uncle Brandon need to get Tilly to the hotel. Pops and Gams are ready for some rest, too."

"Chip, why don't you go put on your pajamas?" Aunt Sarah said. "I'll tuck you in before we go."

"Not *now*," Chip whined. "Charlie's not in his pajamas yet."

"Charlie's a little older than you are, honey," Aunt Sarah explained.

"Well, I don't want to go until he does," Chip said, folding his arms across his chest.

"Charlie," Mom said, "run up and put your pj's on now."

"But, Mom," I protested, "Dad said I could stay up a little longer." Just because it was Chip's bedtime didn't mean it was mine.

"You don't have to go to bed yet, just put your pj's on."

"If Charlie's staying up, can I?" Chip begged.

Aunt Sarah looked at Mom.

Mom shrugged. "It's okay with me," she said. "Maybe they'll sleep later in the morning."

"I doubt it," Aunt Sarah said. "But it's your house."

Chip gave them all good-night hugs, and we went up to my room. He opened his bag and dumped all his clothes on the air mattress.

"Come on, Chip," I said. "If you're going to sleep on my bed, you can't put your stuff where I'm supposed to sleep."

He wasn't listening. He was staring at my dresser. He bounced across the air mattress and picked up my brand-new Buck Meson Transport Module.

"Cool! What's this?" he said, waving it back and forth in the air like it was flying.

"No, Chip! Put that down!"

"Okay, okay," he said.

I took it from him and set it gently back on the dresser.

"Can I at least look at it?"

"Just look at it, don't touch it. And hurry up. I'm almost ready to go back downstairs."

Chip changed into his pj's as fast as he could and ran out of the room. When I heard him pounding down the stairs, I took the Buck Meson Transport

Module and put it in the big bottom drawer of my desk. It would be safe there.

We played with the LEGOs in the family room for a while. At nine-thirty Mom came in and told Chip it was time to go to bed. He announced that he didn't want to go up until I did. He and my mom went back and forth, until finally she got me to go upstairs with him.

"You can come back down after he falls asleep," Mom said to me privately.

◆ ◆ ◆

I lay there on the air mattress waiting for Chip to fall asleep. He wanted to talk, but I told him I was too tired. I was afraid talking would keep him awake even longer.

Finally I saw his eyes close.

As soon as I was sure he was asleep, I tiptoed out and went downstairs. Matt was playing a video game on the computer and didn't want to be bothered. Dad was helping Mom in the kitchen.

"Where's Uncle Ron?" I asked.

"In the garage," Dad said. "Getting something ready for tomorrow."

"The rocket launcher?" I asked.

"I think so," said Mom.

"Can I go see?"

"Okay. But put on your shoes and jacket," Mom said. "And don't be long."

I slipped on my sneakers at the door, grabbed my fleece, and went outside. When I opened the side door of the garage, Uncle Ron was at the workbench cutting something with a saw.

"What are you doing?" I asked.

He looked up and smiled. "Hey, big guy! I'm working on the launch pad for tomorrow. You want to help?"

"Sure!" I said.

"Okay," he said. "Take these plastic tubes and measure out two twelve-inch sections. Mark them on the tube with this marker. You know the rule: Measure twice, cut once. You don't want to cut until you're sure you've got it right."

I could do that. One thing I really liked about Uncle Ron was that he treated me like I was just a person, not some dumb little kid who couldn't do anything.

I measured out the pieces while he kept cutting.

"Here," I said, holding them up.

"Perfect! Put them right here on the bench."

"How does the rocket work?"

"Air pressure," Uncle Ron answered.

"What do you mean?"

"When you put water in the rocket and pump a lot of air into it, the water shoots out of the bottom and pushes the rocket up."

"I don't get it," I said.

"Here, I'll show you," Uncle Ron said. He went over to the

utility sink in the garage, stuck his head under the faucet, and took a big swig of water. Then he turned toward me with his cheeks bulging and smacked both cheeks with his open hands. Water sprayed all over.

I laughed. "Stupific!" I said. "Let me try."

Uncle Ron held me up while I stuck my head under the faucet. When my mouth was full, he put me back down on the ground.

"Just stand there and I'll launch the water," he said. Standing behind me, he set his hands on either side of my puffed-up cheeks. "Five...four...three... two," he counted.

But before he could slap my cheeks, I started laughing and the water came pouring out of my mouth. My pj's were soaked.

"What are you two doing?"

It was my dad. We hadn't heard him open the door.

Uncle Ron and I cracked up.

"I...was just teaching Charlie about...rocket

propulsion," Uncle Ron gasped, still laughing.

Dad shook his head. "I'm not sure you two should be left alone together. Charlie, can you come back inside now?"

"I'm helping Uncle Ron."

"I think you've helped him enough. Any more and you might drown. Chip is awake and says he can't sleep until you go back upstairs."

"Dad! I don't want to!"

"I need your help," he said. "Remember, we talked about this."

"You go ahead, Charlie, and help your cousin," Uncle Ron said. "I'm almost done with this anyway."

I turned and headed out of the garage.

"You're a good dude, Charlie," Uncle Ron said as I left.

When I got up to my room, Chip was sitting up in bed waiting for me. I ignored him and changed into some dry pajamas.

"Where were you?" he asked. "How come you're all wet?"

"Just lie down," I muttered. "I'm going to sleep now."

I was tired. I called Ginger and she trotted in, but instead of lying down with me on the air mattress, she jumped up on my bed.

"No, Ginger. Down here!" She turned around three times and plopped down at the end of the bed.

"Awesome!" Chip said, snuggling under my bedspread. "Ginger's going to sleep with me."

I pulled up the covers on the air mattress and thought about my first definition of family: "A bunch of people you have to live with and share with, even when you don't want to."

So far, it was still the perfect definition.

9

A Long Day

Early on Thanksgiving morning, Chip bounded off the bed and landed right on top of me.

"Hey!" I said, only half awake. "Stop it!"

"Let's wrestle, Charlie!" he said. "I bet I can beat you!"

"Get off!" I pushed him away. Ginger was hanging her head over the side of the bed, watching me be attacked.

"I'm Buck Meson!" Chip yelled.

"Buck Meson doesn't attack sleeping people," I muttered.

"He does now!" Chip said.

I headed to the bathroom. Chip followed me down the hall. I slipped in and shut the door.

"Can I come in?" he yelled.

"No," I said. I did my business and washed my hands. Chip knocked really loud.

"Can I come in now?" he asked.

"No. I'll be out in a minute." When I saw the knob turn, I grabbed it so he couldn't open the door. Then I heard him say, "Hey, the doorknob came off!"

I twisted the doorknob on my side and it came off in my hand.

Not again!

"Stick it back in so I can get out," I said. "I can't open the door!"

He didn't say anything for a second. Then he started to laugh. "You're locked in the bathroom?"

"Yeah," I said. "Open the door!"

"Hey, everybody! Charlie's locked in the bathroom!" I could hear Chip dancing around outside, chanting, "Charlie's locked in the bathroom, Charlie's locked in the bathroom!"

"Chip!" I pounded on the door.

I heard him call down the stairs. "Aunt Gloria! Charlie's locked in the bathroom!"

He was laughing his perfect little turkey head off. Finally, I heard Matt call from his bedroom, "Chip, shut up!" He was obviously still trying to sleep.

Then I heard footsteps coming up the stairs. Little footsteps.

The Squid.

"What's wrong?" she asked.

"Charlie's locked in the bathroom!" Chip said. "He can't get out and I have the doorknob."

"Mabel!" I yelled. "Let me out! It's not funny!"

"Yes, it is!" Chip crowed. "HEY, CHARLIE'S LOCKED IN THE BATHROOM!"

"We need to let him out," the Squid said. "Give me the doorknob."

"No," Chip said. "This is fun. Let's leave him in there a little longer."

"Give it to me!" Mabel shouted. "I know how to do it."

I heard the doorknob go in, so I put my knob

back on and opened the door. The Squid was standing there looking up at me. Chip was smiling. The Squid knew I was mad.

"You were locked in!" Chip said.

"Very funny." I pushed past them and headed back to my room.

It was going to be a long day.

◆ ◆ ◆

When I got downstairs, Mom and Aunt Sarah and Gams were in the kitchen cooking. Pops was there, too, chopping carrots at the kitchen table. The potatoes were already mashed, ready for Dad to make his famous mashed potato casserole.

It's excellent—it has pounds and pounds of cheese in it.

I peeked into the dining room. Dad was setting up an extra table at the end of our big dining table. Mom always put two tablecloths over them so they looked like one really long table stretching all the way to the big picture window in the front of the house.

Uncle Ron was still asleep on the couch in the

family room. His left arm was hanging down, with his big, meaty hand lying on the floor. His snores sounded like the roars of a *Tyrannosaurus rex*.

I stood staring at him for a while. He looked like he hadn't shaved in a couple of days, and he was still wearing the T-shirt he'd had on the night before.

One of his eyes opened, and he raised an eyebrow. He snorted and rubbed his face. "Quit bugging me, big guy," he grumbled. "I need my beauty rest."

And then, before I could say anything, he reached out and grabbed me by my waist. He pulled me over to him, rubbing my face against his whiskers.

"AAAAAAAAH!" I yelled. "Stop it, Uncle Ron!" But I didn't really mind, even though his beard was really rough and scratchy.

Chip came running in. "Hey! What're you guys doing?"

"I'm teaching him a lesson about bothering uncles," Uncle Ron said, letting me go.

Chip leapt onto Uncle Ron. "Do that to me!" he shouted. Uncle Ron turned him upside down, gave him a big squeeze, then lowered him to the floor.

"Okay, you guys," he groaned. "Leave me alone until I get some coffee."

"Charlie and Chip," my dad called. "Come eat your breakfast and let your uncle get dressed."

Chip and I went back into the kitchen and ate some cereal. The Squid had already finished hers and was making little turkeys out of toilet paper rolls and construction paper feathers for everyone's place setting at the table. When Uncle Ron came in and sat down, I hung around, hoping he would say we could build the rocket, but I could tell it wasn't going to happen soon, since he was barely moving. Still, we had plenty of time. Dinner wasn't until three o'clock.

Over by the stove, I saw a bowl covered with a towel. I lifted the towel and touched the big gooey pile of dough with one finger.

"Are these the yeast rolls?" I asked.

Gams smiled. "You bet."

"They're my favorite," I said.

Chip was right behind me, peering in. "They're my favorite, too. Even *more* my favorite."

"Glad you like them, boys," Gams said. "I just punched the dough. You'd better put the cover back on or it won't rise."

I wished Chip was some dough, so I could punch him.

Uncle Ron was still sitting at the table, having a second cup of coffee and talking with my dad. The Squid was busy with her toilet-roll turkeys. Matt was still sleeping. Everywhere I went, Chip was right behind me.

Except when Mom told me to take out the garbage. Of course Chip wouldn't want to help with that!

"But that's Matt's chore," I said.

"Just help me out, Charlie. I need these bags out of the way now."

I was coming back from the big garbage bins on the side of the garage when Chip stuck his head out the back door.

"Charlie, we're coming out! Uncle Ron's going to help us build the rocket!"

Us?

10

Extremely Tired of Waiting

Chip burst out the door, with Uncle Ron behind him. "We'll get started now," Chip said, like he was in charge of everything.

In the garage, I saw that Uncle Ron had finished the launcher the night before. He'd joined all the pieces of plastic tubing together with little connectors to make a sort of platform—it looked really spectacular. Fabulous. Spectabulous.

"I've set everything out over here on the workbench," Uncle Ron said, pointing to some large plastic soda bottles and a stack of cardboard. We cut the cardboard into fins, and then used some poster board to make a pointy nose cone. Finally we cut up one of the bottles and put it on top of the other one. It looked like a rocket!

"Wait," Uncle Ron said. "I forgot about paint. Hey, Charlie, hasn't your dad got some around here?"

"I think so," I said. "What kind do we need?"

"I know about different kinds of paint," Chip announced like some kind of paint expert. "We need the kind that will stick to plastic."

"Anything's fine," Uncle Ron said. "We're just a bunch of morons setting off a water rocket."

"Or bozos," I said.

"Or bo-zons," Uncle Ron said.

I laughed out loud. "Bozon" was a great word.

We looked through the shelves and found a can of black spray paint. "Let's take this outside," Uncle Ron said. "I'd better do the painting. If you guys get paint all over yourselves, your mothers will kill all of us."

We watched as Uncle Ron sprayed the entire rocket. He sprayed the toe of his boot by accident.

But the rocket looked truly, completely stupific!

"Can we shoot it off now?" Chip said. "Can I shoot it first?"

"Not now," Uncle Ron said. "We have to wait for the paint to dry."

"But then can I go first?" Chip asked.

If I had had a large rocket that would hold a seven-year-old, I would've stuck my perfect little turkey cousin in it and sent him to a distant galaxy.

"We'll see," Uncle Ron said.

Why didn't Uncle Ron just tell Chip no?

Why didn't ANYONE ever tell him no?

◆ ◆ ◆

I kept checking on the rocket to see if it was dry.

Chip kept following me.

I kept keeping my mouth shut.

Finally, after forever, the paint was dry. I went back inside with Chip right behind me and found Uncle Ron sprawled on one end of the couch.

Uncle Brandon was sitting on the other end, doing something with his phone. My dad was in the big chair. They were all watching a football game. "Uncle Ron, it's dry," I said. "Can we shoot it off now?"

"Okay," Uncle Ron said, stretching his arms over his head. "Let's put it in the car and we'll head over to the school yard."

"Yippee!" Chip said.

I tore through the kitchen and headed toward the back door.

"Where are you going?" Mom asked.

"To the school to set off the rocket," I said. "It's all ready."

"Not now, Charlie. It's time for you and your dad to go pick up Mrs. Walcott."

"But Mom, can't we shoot the rocket off first? It won't take that long."

Buck Meson would never have to get his mom's permission to shoot off a rocket!

Mom shook her head. "I told Mrs. Walcott we'd pick her up early so she'd have time to visit with people before dinner. She's probably already sitting by the door waiting. And Charlie, you know how much she loves it when you come over."

I like Mrs. Walcott, too. She has to use a walker, which she calls her "Maserati." Dad cracked up the first time she said it because that's the name of a fancy sports car. She has this great accent, since she's from Jamaica. I love listening to her talk.

Once she asked me if I ever got in trouble at school and I told her about the time I accidentally hit Mrs. Burke in the head with a sneaker. She told me that she'd spent a lot of time in the principal's office when she was a little girl.

"Why?" I'd asked her.

"De office more interesting dan de classroom," she'd said, letting out her high-pitched little chuckle.

I liked Mrs. Walcott, but I really wanted to fire the rocket. "Please, Mom. Let us go shoot the rocket really fast," I begged. "Then we'll go get her right after."

"The rocket can wait," Mom said. "Mrs. Walcott cannot."

Boogers.

I went back to Uncle Ron and told him we'd have to wait.

"No problem, Charlie." He plopped back down on the couch. "That way I can watch the rest of the first half."

Just as Dad and I were going out the door, Uncle Brandon called, "Hey, do you guys want to take Chip?"

NO! I thought.

"Sure," Dad said.

"Get your jacket, Chipster," Uncle Brandon called. "You're going with Charlie and Uncle Jim."

Boogers. Boogers. Boogers. Boogers. Boogers.

◆ ◆ ◆

Chip and I climbed into the backseat and Dad pulled out of the driveway. I just stared out the window while Dad explained to Chip where we were going.

"Why do we have to go get her?" Chip asked.

"Mrs. Walcott is one of Aunt Gloria's patients," Dad said. "She can't drive herself."

"Why is she coming over?"

"Because it's Thanksgiving and she doesn't have any family nearby."

"Oh," said Chip.

When we pulled up in front of Mrs. Walcott's house, Dad got out. "Let's go," he said. "Chip, you stay in the car for just a minute. We'll be right back."

On the front porch, Dad let me ring the doorbell. Right away, the locks rattled on the other side and the door opened. Mrs. Walcott was wearing a blue hat that matched her blue coat.

"Well, I see you're all ready!" my dad said.

"Me tek six hours fi get to de door!" she said. Then she grinned at me. "T'anks for coming, Charlie. Why you no carry de Maserati? Me sure you handsome papa will help de ol' lady down dese stairs."

While Dad was helping Mrs. Walcott into the front seat, I put the walker in the trunk and climbed into the backseat.

"She's really old!" Chip whispered. He almost looked scared.

As soon as my dad got Mrs. Walcott settled and her seat belt buckled, she turned around and peered at Chip. "What you name, little man?" she asked him.

"Chip," he mumbled.

"Nice to meet you, Cheep," she said. Then she gave me a little wink. "You mind spending de evening wit de crabby ol' lady?"

"Um, no," Chip said.

"Dat's good," Mrs. Walcott said. "Because me no have a nice dinner in donkey's years. And it look like I'm coming—unless Charlie's father decide fi lef me at de animal shelter wit de other ol' crittahs." She winked at me and I smiled back.

"No chance of that," said Dad.

◆ ◆ ◆

Back at home, after we got Mrs. Walcott settled in the kitchen, I ran into the family room to tell Uncle

Ron we could go fire off the rocket. Before he could answer, the front doorbell rang and Ginger started barking.

"Somebody get it!" Mom yelled from the kitchen. "It must be the Gritzbachs."

Not the Gritzbachs!

The Squid raced toward the door.

"Let's go, Uncle Ron." I pulled on his sleeve.

"Let's go," said Chip, the perfect little copycat.

"Wait a minute," Dad said. "They're already putting out the appetizers." He looked at his watch. "We're going to sit down and eat in an hour."

"Come on, Dad," I pleaded. "We'll be right back. It won't take very long. Right, Uncle Ron?"

"We could probably get there and back in half an hour," he said.

"Good," I said. "Let's go."

"Ron," Dad said. "It'll take you ten or fifteen minutes just to get to the school."

"No, it won't!" I shouted.

"Cool it, Charlie," Dad said.

And then the Squid led Mr. and Mrs. Gritzbach
into the room just as my mom came in from the
kitchen.

Dad went to the stairs and yelled for Matt to
come down.

Mrs. Gritzbach handed my mom a covered dish.
"I brought one of my specialties—creamed brussels
sprouts."

Brussels sprouts! The smelliest, most disgusting
vegetable on the
planet!

"Thank you
so much," Mom
said, giving
Mrs. Gritzbach
a little one-arm
hug.

"They
just need a
little heating
up," Mrs.
Gritzbach
said.

They didn't need a little heating up. They needed a little throwing away!

My mom went in the kitchen with the brussels sprouts and came back out with Mrs. Walcott, Gams, and Aunt Sarah, who was holding Tilly. Mrs. Gritzbach smiled at me and shook my hand. "Nice to see you, Charlie," she said.

"Hi," I answered. Then I turned to her husband. "Hello, Mr. Gritzbach."

"Hello," he grunted.

Suddenly, Chip stepped forward. "Hello, Mr. and Mrs. Gritzbach. I'm Chip—Charlie's cousin. It's nice to meet you."

Mr. Gritzbach nodded. "You, too," he said, shaking Chip's hand. Then he looked at me like *I* was the turkey.

Grown-ups always thought Chip was soooo polite! But I had other things on my mind.

"Uncle Ron," I said, "can we *please*—?"

"Charlie," Mom interrupted. "It's nearly time for

dinner. You and Mabel run upstairs and change into nice clothes."

"But we're going to launch the rocket!" I moaned.

"Upstairs. Get your clothes on now," Mom said. "The rocket can wait."

The rocket could not wait! The rocket was extremely tired of waiting!

"We'll go to the school really fast," I said. "We'll be back in plenty of time to change."

Mom gave me one of her don't-push-your-luck looks.

"We'll figure something out, Charlie," Uncle Ron said. "Better do what your mom says."

"I've already got my good clothes on," Chip announced to the universe.

11

A Rocket?
On T'anksgiving?

I raced up the stairs, and the Squid ran up after me. "I want to see the rocket, too!" she squeaked.

I scooted into my room, ripped off my jeans and T-shirt, and yanked open the drawer that held my nice shirts with buttons on them. I pulled one on. I found a pair of pants in the closet and put those on. I tucked my shirt in, then put my sneakers back on and raced down the stairs.

My mom took one look at my feet. "I said *nice* clothes, Charlie," she said. "Go put on your dress shoes."

Not dress shoes!

I ran back upstairs and nearly collided with the Squid in the hallway. I dodged past her and dashed into my room. I hadn't worn my good shoes since forever and had to empty out half the closet before I found them. As I put them on, I looked around my room.

I had destroyed it in thirty seconds! I'd have to clean it later.

I hurtled back downstairs. Mom and the other women were in the kitchen and the men were standing around in the family room eating appetizers and talking.

"Now can we go?" I asked Uncle Ron.

Dad looked at his watch. "I don't know, you guys. It's getting kind of late. You won't have time to get there and back before we start eating."

"But we have to shoot it off!" I said.

"We *have* to shoot it off," Chip echoed.

"We *have* to shoot it off!" the Squid double-echoed.

"Okay," Uncle Ron said. "We'll shoot it off here."

Dad gave his brother a funny look. "Here?"

"Don't worry," my uncle said. "It'll be fine."

"I don't think there's enough room in the backyard," Dad said.

"There's enough room!" I said.

"We'll launch it in the street," Uncle Ron said. "There's not much traffic today and it'll be safe. It's not windy. The rocket will just go up and then come straight down."

Dad screwed up his face and rubbed his eyes, which he does when he's making a hard decision. He looked toward the kitchen to see if Mom was listening.

"Okay," he said softly. "Go now and get it over with."

"It'll be fine, Jimmy," Uncle Ron reassured Dad.

"It better be," Dad said.

"What kind of rocket are you talking about?" Mr. Gritzbach asked.

"The kids made a soda-bottle rocket," Dad said.

"Sounds exciting," Pops said.

"Any danger of explosions?" Mr. Gritzbach asked.

"Naw," Uncle Ron said. "It's just water. No problem."

Finally! We were actually going to shoot off the rocket!

"I'm first," Chip announced.

"Uncle Ron gets to choose," the Squid said, giving Chip a dirty look.

"Let's go set everything up," Uncle Ron said.

Mom and the others in the kitchen didn't seem to notice us when we passed through the first time. They were too busy with the last-minute cooking. Mrs. Walcott was sitting at the table, arranging cookies on a tray. The kitchen was filled with the smell of the turkey roasting and Gams was brushing butter over the tops of the yeast rolls.

But when we came back in from the garage to fill the rocket, Mom turned around. "What's going on?" she asked suspiciously.

Trick question! No good answer!

"We're just going to borrow the sink for a minute," Uncle Ron said.

"We don't need any interruptions in the kitchen right now," Mom said.

"We have to fill up the rocket!" Chip said.

I stuck the rocket under the faucet and turned on the water, before Mom kicked us out.

"A rocket? On T'anksgiving?" Mrs. Walcott grinned. "Dat a big fun!"

"You're not going to launch it now, are you?" Mom asked.

Another trick question!

"We're not going to the school," I said quickly. "We're going to shoot it off outside. We'll just do it once."

"Twice," Chip said.

"We'll do it in the street," Uncle Ron said.

"I don't think that's a good idea," Mom said. She was holding a big metal spoon in her hand and she looked fairly dangerous.

Dad stuck his head in the door. "I told them it would be okay, Gloria."

Mom shook her head. "All right, but don't make

a mess in here. And don't take long. It's almost time to put the rolls in the oven."

"Hurry up, you guys," Dad said.

Matt suddenly appeared. "Don't worry, Dad," he said. "I'll supervise."

"Now I *am* worried," Dad said, but he was smiling.

We kids followed Uncle Ron out the kitchen door, and he opened up the back part of his truck. He pulled out a bicycle pump and handed it to the Squid. I was still holding the rocket.

"Matt and Chip, I need your help in the garage for a minute," Uncle Ron said. After a few seconds they came out carrying the launcher.

"Let's go, guys!" Uncle Ron called.

"And girl!" the Squid announced. *"G-I-R-L!"*

"Yeah, most definitely," Uncle Ron said. "And *g-i-r-l.*"

We paraded out to the street. It was almost two o'clock in the afternoon, and it was completely quiet. Perfect for setting off a rocket.

"Everyone be careful now," Uncle Ron said. "We're going to put the rocket on this tube here and make sure it's pointed straight up. Then we'll pump until there's enough air in the rocket. When everything is ready, we'll pull back on this string."

"I'll pull the string," Chip announced.

Uncle Ron stopped and looked at Chip. "If things go okay, we'll do it a couple of times. But since we're guests at Charlie's house, we'll let him pull it first."

"But I said it first," Chip protested.

"We'll let Charlie pull first," Uncle Ron said.

"That's not fair," Chip said.

I looked at Matt, then at the Squid. We all said it together: "Life's not fair!"

Uncle Ron laughed. Chip frowned and made a face.

Finally, Chip wasn't going to get his way!

"We'll all pump," Uncle Ron instructed us. "Everybody gets ten pumps. You want a turn, Matt?"

"I'm good." Matt folded his arms across his chest and watched us work with a smirk on his face.

I heard the front door open. Pops stepped out and held the door for Mr. Gritzbach. Mrs. Walcott was standing just inside with her walker. The two old men stood on the porch, leaning back against the open storm door so she could see. Mom and Aunt Sarah and Gams and Mrs. Gritzbach and Dad were all still inside. I guess they didn't care about the Thanksgiving rocket.

"Almost ready, Pops?" I yelled. He nodded, grinned, and gave me a thumbs up. Even Mr. Gritzbach had a sort of smile on his face.

We pumped ten times each, which made forty. "Wait a sec," Uncle Ron said. "It's leaning a little.

Let me make sure it's pointing straight up in the air." He started toward the launcher.

But Chip got there first. "This is the string you pull, right?" he said.

"No!" Uncle Ron said.

Chip pulled the string.

The rocket shot off the launcher. It spewed water out, spraying all of us.

But it did not go straight up in the air.

Instead, the rocket took a turn to the left and zoomed across the yard, staying about six feet above the ground. It seemed like it was flying about two hundred miles an hour.

Right toward our front door.

12

Steam Coming Out of Her Ears

It happened so quickly, I barely had time to think. For a split second I thought the rocket was going to slam into Pops and Mr. Gritzbach.

But it zipped right by them.

Right through the open front door.

Right over Mrs. Walcott, who ducked down over her walker just in time.

Then we heard a crash and a scream.

Uh-oh.

We all looked at each other.

"Oh man!" Uncle Ron moaned and ran toward the door. He leapt up the steps and sprinted through the front door. "Excuse me, gentlemen," Uncle Ron said as he ran past Pops and Mr. Gritzbach.

I was right behind him.

Pops and Mr. Gritzbach had weird looks on their faces, which I guess is the kind of look you get when you're almost hit by a rocket.

Mrs. Walcott had her hands folded together and a little grin on her face.

Gams and Mrs. Gritzbach were sitting on the sofa in the living room, gripping their punch glasses with both hands. Aunt Sarah was holding Tilly. Their eyes looked like they were going to pop out of their heads.

Mom was standing in the middle of the room, hands on her hips. There were three or four plates of food scattered on the floor. The coffee table was lying on its side and cheese straws and carrot sticks were scattered all around.

The rocket was lying in the corner with a big dent in the nose cone.

Dad was standing in the doorway to the kitchen with both hands over his face.

Aunt Sarah took Tilly out of the room.

"My goodness," Gams said.

"What happened?" Mrs. Gritzbach asked.

"Whoops," Uncle Ron said. "Everybody okay?"

"Do it again, nuh?" Mrs. Walcott asked.

I looked at Mom. If we'd been in a cartoon, there would've been little puffs of steam coming out of her ears.

I picked up the crumpled rocket. Uncle Ron motioned that I should take it outside, then he got down on his knees and started to clean up the plates and food. By this time, everybody had come in from the front yard and was standing by the door—Mr. Gritzbach, Pops, the Squid, and Matt. I didn't see Chip, who had started everything.

"Amaaaaazing!" Matt observed.

Mom headed straight toward Dad, grabbed him by the arm, and dragged him into the kitchen. We heard the back door open and shut.

And then a miracle happened. Matt, who usually just watched things happen, started helping Uncle Ron clear things away. He set the coffee table back up and wiped it with a big handful of paper napkins. "I'll go get some more appetizers," he said, disappearing into the kitchen.

In a few seconds he came back with a plate of cheese and crackers.

I knew it was still really Matt, because he was

stuffing some crackers in his mouth as he put down the plate.

I took the rocket outside, went into the street, and picked up the launcher. I headed around the house, and Chip followed me.

"I didn't know it was going to do that," he said.

"You didn't listen to Uncle Ron!" I said.

The perfect little turkey had almost mowed down the whole family. And the guests.

Mom and Dad were standing in the driveway by the garage arguing with each other. When Chip saw them, he stopped and went back toward the front yard. I kept going.

"It's not Uncle Ron's fault," I said.

"Not now, Charlie," Mom said.

"He told us not to fire it, but Chip—"

"Not now!" Mom repeated. Dad shook his head, warning me not to say anything.

The way Mom looked at me, I could tell she thought it was my fault, too. But there wasn't much point in trying to explain. Sometimes, explanations are impossible. Especially when you're talking to a marine sergeant mad scientist mom. Especially when people had almost died in a catastrophic water rocket accident.

I went back inside. The kitchen was filled with the smells of all different kinds of delicious food, but the most beautiful smell of all came from Gams's rolls. They had just come out of the oven. Gams had put them in a basket wrapped up in a napkin.

Guess who was standing right next to the basket, tossing a hot roll from hand to hand?

"Chip!" I yelled. "You aren't supposed to eat those yet!"

"They're my favorite," Chip said, taking a bite.

"Save some for everybody else."

"There's a lot," he said.

Just then, I heard Matt's voice. "Hey, Charlie, come here!"

"No rolls until dinnertime!" I said and gave Chip a Buck Meson electron stare.

Matt came up behind me. "Charlie!" he said softly. "Up to my room. Important Bumpers meeting. Now."

"Can I come?" Chip asked, still chewing on the roll.

"Only if your name is Bumpers," Matt said. "Sorry, Chip. It'll just take a minute. Let's go, Charlie."

I wondered what Matt had in mind. I followed him up the stairs, with the Squid on my heels. Matt led us into his bedroom and closed the door.

13

We Are Ever Vigilant

"Sit on the bed, you guys," Matt said.

"And girl," the Squid said.

We sat on his bed. This was unbelievable! He never invited either of us into his room, especially not me.

"It's time for Operation Perfect Little Turkey," he said.

"What's that?" the Squid asked.

"I hate to admit this, Mabel, but Chip is giving Charlie a really hard time. As his brother and sister, we are the only ones allowed to do that. It's time for us to protect him."

"What do you mean?" I asked.

"I mean we have to make sure that Chip stops bugging you and that you don't keep getting blamed for stuff you didn't do. Mom and Dad are too busy to notice what's really going on, so we'll have to take the law into our own hands."

That sounded pretty interesting.

"Chip doesn't listen," the Squid announced, nodding her head. "He's not a perfect turkey. He's a turkey *butt*."

That was about as bad a word as the Squid would ever say.

"Right, Mabel," Matt said, and he turned back to me. "We are ever vigilant in protecting the rights of the falsely accused, which means you, Charlie. Mabel and I have to keep an eye on Chip to make sure he does not continue to be a turkey butt."

"He's driving me crazy," I said. "He almost killed everyone with the rocket, and I think he's going to eat all of Gams's rolls. I'm afraid I won't get any."

"The rolls are not a problem," Matt said. "When they're passed around the table to us, we'll each take some extras and keep them in our laps. Then we can share them with each other if one of us comes up empty-handed."

"Okay," the Squid said. She was excited about being included in a plan with her big brothers.

"What are our other objectives?" Matt asked. He was beginning to sound like Buck Meson!

"Well," I said, thinking about what else Chip might do. "I just hope I get some whipped cream on my pumpkin pie. Remember last summer when we were making strawberry shortcake and Chip used up the whole can of whipped cream?"

"That was *him?*" Matt asked. "What a sneak!"

"Yeah!" I said. "He squirted the whole can on his strawberries."

"Not today," Matt said. "You'll have as much whipped cream as you want."

"Can I have some?" the Squid asked.

"All the Bumpers children will have whipped cream," Matt announced. "When it's time for dessert, we have to be the first up to clear the table before anyone else gets in the kitchen. Follow my lead. Do you understand?"

We both nodded.

"What else?" Matt asked.

"Well," I went on, "the only other thing I'm really worried about is getting to watch the Buck Meson special when it comes on."

"Don't worry about that," Matt said. "Even though it's a dumb show, I'll make sure you get to see it. Anything else?"

I thought of one more problem.

"What if I have to eat Mrs. Gritzbach's brussels sprouts?"

"You're on your own with that, Charlie," Matt said. "I can't stand them either."

"Neither can I," the Squid said.

"Charlie," Matt said, "just remember the first rule in dealing with younger relatives: 'Don't let them bug you.'"

"It's hard," I said.

"You can do it," he said. "You're smart."

Wow. Matt had never told me *that* before.

"Though not as smart as me," he added, grinning.

Just then we heard Dad calling up the stairs. "Matt! Charlie! Mabel! Down here right now!"

"Let's go, Team Bumpers," said Matt. "Our mission is to help our bozo brother."

"Thanks, guys," I said.

"Guy and *girl*," the Squid corrected me. "They both begin with *g* but they are not the same."

We piled back down the stairs and headed for the Thanksgiving table.

14

What on Earth Do You Think You're Doing?

Mom had labeled each of the Squid's toilet-roll turkeys with the name of the person who was supposed to sit at each place and arranged them on the table. I walked around until I found mine. Mrs. Gritzbach was on one side of me.

Guess whose toilet-roll turkey was on the other side?

Right. Chip, the Perfect Little Turkey himself. While everyone else was busy finding their seats, I saw Matt reach into the basket of rolls. He handed a couple to the Squid and kept some for himself.

When they sat at their places, they slipped the rolls into their laps. Holy moly! They were really doing it!

The Squid looked like she had a secret she really wanted to tell and could hardly wait. Matt had a smirk on his face.

"I'm so glad I'm next to you," Mrs. Gritzbach said to me as she unfolded her napkin. "You can help me serve."

That's when I noticed what was right in front of her.

The brussels sprouts.

I hoped she would let me serve myself. Then I could serve myself nothing.

Mom and Aunt Sarah came in from the kitchen and Aunt Sarah set Tilly in the high chair next to her. Ginger settled down under the table, which is where she likes to be in case anyone drops something by accident.

"Let's give thanks," Mom said.

We all held hands and bowed our heads. It was quiet for a moment, which was amazing, since there were fifteen of us. Even Ginger was quiet. I wondered what dogs are thankful for.

My dad began to name some things he was thankful for. He's usually funny, but this time he didn't make any jokes or wisecracks. I could tell everyone was really listening. While Dad was talking, I thought about Mrs. Burke's assignment. I wished I had just written something simple about families in the first place. Like listing all my relatives—a mom and dad and brother and sister and grandparents and aunts and uncles and cousins.

Okay, maybe not my cousin.

"Let's eat!" Uncle Ron said.

Dad carved the turkey. Pops placed a couple of slices on the plates and passed them to Mom, who loaded on potatoes and dressing and cranberry relish and other stuff. Then Mom handed the plates over to Mrs. Gritzbach, who spooned on some brussels sprouts.

In a little while, I could tell that the next plate would stop at my place. It had been around the table gathering food, including the cranberry relish, which I did not like, and my dad's mashed potato casserole, which I did. When the plate passed by Matt and the Squid, I saw them each reach down, pick up a roll off their laps, and slip it on my plate.

It came to me before it reached Mrs. Gritzbach, and I quickly put it down in front of me. *Good,* I thought. *No room for brussels sprouts.*

"I seem to have missed you, Charlie," Mrs. Gritzbach said, and she dumped five brussels sprouts on my already crowded plate.

That was more brussels sprouts than I'd eaten in my entire nine years of life.

"Please start the rolls around, Matt," Mom said. He and the Squid each took one, then passed the basket. When it reached Aunt Sarah, she said, "Wow! These rolls are disappearing fast!"

"Well," Gams said, "the cook takes it as a compliment. I guess I just didn't make enough."

When the basket came around the table, Chip took the last roll. That figured.

But I didn't care. I already had two on my plate, thanks to Matt and the Squid.

As we ate, Aunt Sarah started to tell about how when she was little, Mom, her older sister, had convinced her she could dye her hair with green food coloring and that it would wash out right away.

Except it didn't.

Gams laughed and said they'd had to cut all of Aunt Sarah's hair off.

"You looked like an alien!" Pops said. "Even your scalp was green."

"You were so mean!" Aunt Sarah said to Mom.

"Because you were a horrible little sister!" Mom was smiling when she said it, so I knew she was teasing.

"Not as horrible as Ron," Dad said.

Uncle Ron laughed out loud. "What are you talking about, dude? You were the meanest big brother of all time! Remember the time you got me stuck up on the roof?"

I had heard all of those stories before, but I loved

hearing them again. Everybody was laughing and enjoying the food, and saying how good everything tasted.

The turkey and the mashed potatoes and the rolls were stupific. Spectabulous. I even ate a little of the cranberry relish and one of the sprouts, just to be polite. It was not stupific. Or spectabulous. It was horrible. And as the rest of the food on my plate disappeared, the other four brussels sprouts became more and more noticeable.

I was trying to figure out a way to get rid of the sprouts without hurting Mrs. Gritzbach's feelings when I felt something brush against my foot. Ginger was crawling around under the table, looking to see if anyone had dropped anything.

I wondered if dogs liked brussels sprouts.

When no one was looking, I slipped one off my plate and held it under the table. Right away, I could feel Ginger's muzzle in my hand. She took the brussels sprout!

One more down! Three to go!

I slid another one under the table. I felt Ginger's mouth on my hand again and the sprout disappeared. She was going to eat all of them!

The next time, the brussels sprout slipped out of my hand. I looked down and saw all the brussels sprouts on the floor. Ginger hadn't eaten any of them!

"Hey," Chip said, peering under the table. "Charlie dropped his brussels sprouts."

Mom gave me a look.

"I just spilled a couple," I said. "I'll get them."

I grabbed my napkin and knelt down on the floor. I put the squishy sprouts in the napkin and crawled out from under the table.

I took the disgusting vegetables and dumped them into the kitchen wastebasket. Then I went back to my seat and sat down. Mrs. Gritzbach picked up

the serving spoon. "Here, Charlie," she said. "There are still a few left."

"I don't...I mean, I..."

She was about to put the last three sprouts on my plate when Mrs. Walcott spoke up.

"Excuse me," she said. "I'd like de rest of de brussels sprouts. Dem taste so good." She held her plate out across the table. "If Charlie don' mind?"

"No," I said. "It's alright."

While Mrs. Gritzbach was ladling the sprouts on her plate, Mrs. Walcott gave me a wink.

When the main meal was almost over, Matt suddenly jumped up from the table. "Everybody stay where you are!" he announced. "The Bumpers children will clear the table."

Mom smiled. Dad said, "Miracles do happen!"

◆ ◆ ◆

I wasn't sure exactly what Matt had in mind, but I started clearing away the plates.

When I took Mrs. Walcott's plate, I saw all the brussels sprouts were still there.

I guess when you get to be older, you can eat whatever you want.

When I went into the kitchen with my third load of plates and platters, Matt was standing by the counter shaking the can of whipped cream.

"Charlie, Mabel," he said. "Come here, quick."

I walked over to Matt and the Squid followed close behind me. Matt leaned his head back, stuck the nozzle in his mouth, and squirted whipped cream right into his mouth. He wiped his lips and grinned. "Okay, Charlie," he said. "Open your mouth and tilt back your head! Hurry!"

Matt stuck the nozzle of whipped cream in my mouth and pushed the button. Before I could swallow, it filled my mouth and ran down my chin.

"That's enough!" I said. Except it sounded like *"Aghghh egughh!"*

"My turn!" the Squid squealed.

Matt handed me the can. "Time to share with your sister."

I grabbed a dish towel and wiped the whipped cream off my face and my nice dress shirt.

The Squid opened her mouth, tilted back her head, and closed her eyes. "I'm ready, Charlie!" she said, sticking out her tongue.

I pressed down the nozzle.

The whipped cream shot out of the can and into the Squid's mouth.

I have always said that the Squid has a big mouth, but actually, it's very small—it didn't hold very much. She started to laugh and whipped cream sprayed out of her mouth.

"It tickles!" she said. Except it sounded like "*Ight gighhhhawz.*"

We passed the can around again.

"What's going on?" Mom said from behind us.

We turned and looked.

She was standing in the doorway. And she was not happy.

All of us still had mouthfuls of whipped cream.

"What on earth do you think you're doing?" she said.

Trick question! No good answer!

The Squid swallowed, then spoke up. "Last time Chip hogged all the whipped cream, so this time we wanted to make sure *we* got some."

"Whose idea was this?"

The Squid and I looked at each other. We weren't going to tell on Matt. We were Team Bumpers.

"Mine," Matt said.

Mom shook her head. "You three are not helping."

"Actually, we did clear the table," Matt observed.

"Well, finish the job, and please try to behave yourselves for a little while longer."

We carried the dessert plates and forks to the dining room and Mom brought out the pies and the can of whipped cream. Dad went into the kitchen and brought out coffee for the grown-ups. Matt, the Squid, and I sat down while Mom cut slices of pie for everyone.

"We're not sure how much whipped cream we have," she said, glaring at us. "So the Bumpers children have graciously volunteered not to have any."

We all just nodded. Uncle Ron turned to my dad and said, "Hey, Jimmy, remember when we used to squirt whipped cream in each other's mouths?"

"That was a riot," Dad said. "Have you kids ever tried that?"

"Once," Matt said.

Mom glared at both Dad and Uncle Ron.

"Dat sound like fun," Mrs. Walcott announced.

"Can I try it?" Chip asked.

"Not today," Aunt Sarah said.

I smiled to myself and ate my pie with no whipped cream.

15

You Mean P-a-i-n

At the end of dinner, all the grown-ups sat around talking like they always do. Just when I thought I'd have to listen to them forever, the phone in the kitchen rang. I ran to answer it.

"I DON'T THINK SO!" said a voice on the other end of the line.

Buck Meson's famous line. It was Tommy.

I glanced at the clock. "Half an hour to Buck Meson liftoff, dude," I said.

"You all ready?" he asked.

"I'm ready, but I hope people leave before the show starts. We have a lot of guests."

"I know!" Tommy said. "I'm at my aunt and uncle's house and there's a million people here. But we're going to go home soon. Then I'll be able watch the special without anyone to bug me."

"I've got someone who's going to bother me no matter what," I said in a low voice. "My cousin Chip."

"Argh! Cousins!" Tommy said. "Families can drive you crazy."

"I know. Families are a big pain." *Except,* I thought, *maybe for Team Bumpers.*

"Right," Tommy said. "I'll call you after the show is over so we can talk about who gets the electron stare."

I hung up and went back to the table to find the grown-ups had finally stopped talking. Pops, Gams, Aunt Sarah, and Uncle Brandon were putting on their coats. The Gritzbachs were standing by the door, saying good-bye to my dad.

Things were working out perfectly—they were leaving just in time for me to watch the show.

Aunt Sarah kissed Chip, and Uncle Brandon gave him a hug. "Be a good guy like you always are," he said.

"We're going to watch Buck Meson," Chip announced.

"Good night, everyone," Aunt Sarah said. "We really enjoyed the dinner."

"Thanks, everyone," Gams said with a big smile. "It was wonderful being together."

"We had a beautiful time," Mrs. Gritzbach said. "Thank you so much for letting us spend the day with your family. You made us feel like we belonged."

"Thank you," grumbled Mr. Gritzbach.

"Let me help you with your coat, Irma," Mom said to Mrs. Walcott. "I'll take you home. Charlie, can you come with us?"

This couldn't happen! I liked Mrs. Walcott and I didn't want to hurt her feelings, but I couldn't miss Buck Meson!

"Charlie wants to watch Buck Meson," the Squid said. "The show's going to start soon."

"Charlie can go with us," Mom said. "He doesn't mind."

Charlie does mind! He minds very much!

"Oh, leave dat boy alone," Mrs. Walcott said with a very definite tone in her voice. "It don' mek sense for him to miss his show." She gave her little chuckle. "But Charlie, if you help de ol' lady get de Maserati in de car, dat will be very kind of you."

"I'll go with you," said Uncle Ron.

"That would be very nice," said Mom. "Thanks, Ron."

"Not a problem," he said, grabbing his jacket.

I put Mrs. Walcott's walker in Mom's car and watched them drive away. Then I hurried back into the house. The Squid and Chip were already in the family room. Dad was listening to music in the living room, so we had the TV to ourselves. I turned it on and punched in the right channel. The show was going to start in fifteen minutes.

I could hardly wait.

Chip got up and stood in front of the screen.

He crouched down, then whirled around and leapt toward me like some sort of kid ninja.

"I'm Buck Meson," he announced, "and you're the bad guy!"

"Sit down, Chip," I said.

"Who's the bad guy in this episode?" he asked.

"I don't know," I said. "Probably Calculus."

Calculus was a sinister mastermind from the Evil Eye galaxy who had once figured out how to get into everyone's bank accounts, taken billions of dollars, and then built a machine to destroy Planet Xanthos. Buck Meson caught him and put him in the Intergalactic Cyberprison, but Calculus programmed the doors of the prison to open with a remote device and he escaped along with all the other super criminals.

Until Buck Meson's electron stare paralyzed him.

"You're Calculus! Hah!" Chip aimed a karate kick at me.

"Stop it, Chip," I said.

He vaulted over the back of the couch and ran

around yelling, "I can't stop! I'm fighting Calculus! I'm the hero, Buck Meson!"

Chip was bonkers. Maybe the sugar and food he'd been eating all day long was suddenly making him a wild man.

"Sit down!" the Squid shouted.

"Okay, okay," Chip said, bounding into my dad's big easy chair. He sat there, bouncing up and down on the seat.

After what seemed like forever, the show started. As soon as the Buck Meson theme song came on,

Chip got up again. "Wait a minute!" he said. "I want to get something!"

"What?" I asked.

"Pause it!" he said. "I'll be right back."

I paused the show. I was getting pretty frustrated.

Chip ran out of the room and came back in with the big jar of Swedish Fish. I couldn't believe it—half of them were gone already! He must have been eating them all day long. He opened the jar, took out a handful, and stuffed them in his mouth.

"Okay," he said. "Start it." He plopped back down and started kicking his legs against the chair. But at least he wasn't talking and I could watch the show.

As the program began, Buck Meson was leaving his planet in the Andromeda Galaxy to visit Earth in his transport module.

"That's just like your model!" Chip shouted. "The one I saw in your room."

"Be quiet!" the Squid said. "Charlie wants to watch the show."

I could tell she was getting mad.

After about ten minutes of the show, Matt stuck his head in the family room.

"Aren't you going to watch with us?" I asked.

"Nope," he said. "I'm going up to my room—to a galaxy far, far away."

Three minutes later, Chip jumped up again. "I have to go the bathroom," he said. "Pause it."

"Just hurry up and go," I said. "You won't miss much."

"Please pause it," he begged. "I don't want to miss anything. And I really have to go."

"Okay," I said, pushing the pause button. "But I'm not waiting long!" Tommy was going to call as soon as it was over and I didn't want him to get ahead of me.

Chip tore up the stairs.

"Chip is a *p-a-n-e*," the Squid said.

"You mean *p-a-i-n*," I said.

We sat there for a moment, staring at the frozen screen. Suddenly the Squid got up. "I want to get my pony pillow," she said. "I'll be right back!"

"Mabel!" I groaned. "Hurry up!"

The Squid scampered up the stairs. Now I was waiting for *two* little kids.

Uncle Ron and Mom had come back and they were in the living room with Dad, listening to music and talking. Matt was in his room, probably with his headphones on. Finally the Squid came hopping back down the stairs and ran in with her pillow.

"Where's Chip?" I asked.

"Still in the bathroom," she said. "You can go ahead and watch. It's okay."

"Are you sure?"

"Yep!" she said.

I hit Play and we went back to watching the show.

It was great—in my opinion the best *Buck Meson* yet. When he got to Earth, he immediately got caught by some intergalactic criminals. And I was right—Calculus was behind it all!

Every once in a while I thought about Chip, but then I figured he just got interested in something else and didn't want to watch anymore.

After about twenty minutes had gone by, Chip still hadn't returned. That seemed a little weird. He'd been bugging me all day, and suddenly he had disappeared.

"Do you think Chip's still in the bathroom?" I asked the Squid.

"I think so," she said.

"That's a long time to be in the bathroom. Do you think he's sick?"

"No," she said. "Let's watch the show."

Something in the way she said that made me look at the Squid more closely. "Why don't you think he's sick?"

"Well, maybe he's a little sick," she said. "But I think he's just in the bathroom."

"What's going on up there?" I heard my dad call. I turned and saw him standing at the bottom of the stairs. "Matt? Charlie?"

"I'm down here," I said. Then I heard it. Someone was screaming and pounding on something.

"What's that?" I glanced over at the Squid. She had the guiltiest look on her face I had ever seen.

"I think Chip's locked in the bathroom," she said.

"Did the doorknob fall off?" I said.

She didn't answer.

"Mabel! Did you take the doorknob?"

Now Mom and Uncle Ron were hurrying up the stairs. We could hear Chip wailing.

"Where's the doorknob?" I asked my sister.

She looked at her pony pillow. I took it from her and stuck my hand down in between the pillow case and the pillow. I felt the doorknob.

"Mabel! What did you do?"

She grabbed her pony pillow and put it over her head.

16

B-A-R-P-H

I headed out of the room with the doorknob in my hand. Just as I got to the stairs, Uncle Ron came running down. He blew by me and I heard the back door slam as he went outside. I figured he was going to his truck to get his tools.

When I got upstairs, I found Mom, Dad, and Matt standing by the bathroom door. Chip was screaming and sobbing on the other side.

"It's okay, Chip," Mom was saying. "We'll get you out in a jiffy. Uncle Ron can get the door open."

"I want Mom!" he wailed.

I squeezed between them, shoved the doorknob in the hole in the door, and gave it a twist. The door opened and there was Chip in the bathroom, standing by the toilet.

In his hands was the Buck Meson Transport Module.

Broken in half.

"You broke my model!" I yelled.

"Not now, Charlie," Dad said.

Not now! When? Chip had destroyed my perfect transport module!

"I don't feel good!" Chip moaned. Neither did I.

Mom gave me a cold look, then took Chip by the hand and led him into my room.

"I don't feel good," he kept saying. "I want my mom."

I heard my mother say, "You're fine now. You just need to calm down."

"I can't," he said hiccupping and sobbing. "I feel bad, I feel—"

And then I heard the unmistakable sound of someone throwing up.

I ran into my room.

I sure didn't want to sleep in my own bed that night.

Or maybe ever.

Mom helped Chip off the bed and back into the bathroom. I stood there looking at Chip's Thanksgiving dinner. The rolls and the whipped cream.

And the Swedish Fish. A lot of them, swimming around in everything else.

And my broken model of the Buck Meson Transport Module.

Buck Meson! The special was still on downstairs! I ran out of my bedroom. Right into Dad.

"Charlie, Matt, Mabel, come with me," he said, in his very serious voice that I never wanted to hear.

"But *Buck Meson*'s on downstairs!" I said.

"I don't care where he is, we need a talk."

"I didn't do anything!" Matt said.

The Squid's mouth was shut in a tight line.

"Come with me," Dad said. "All of you."

"Let me go pause the show," I pleaded.

"Right *now*," Dad said.

He was mad.

Never mess with a mad dad.

He led us into his and mom's bedroom, then closed the door. "Charlie," he said, "did you lock Chip in the bathroom?"

"No, I just had the doorknob."

Dad gave me a confused look. "You just had the doorknob?"

"Yes," I said.

I looked at the Squid. Her bottom lip was trembling.

"How did you get the doorknob?"

I looked at the floor. I didn't really want to tell all this to Dad. It was going to be a very complicated explanation.

"What about you, Matt?" Dad asked. "Didn't you hear Chip calling for help? You were the closest."

"Um…I had my headphones on."

Dad squinted and gave Matt an icy stare. My brother looked at the floor, too.

"What exactly is going on here?" Dad said.

It got really quiet. We could hear the faucet running in the bathroom and Mom talking softly to Chip. I was about to say something, but the Squid spoke first.

"I did it!" she blurted out.

"Did what?" Dad asked.

"I took the doorknob away so Charlie could watch the show!"

"What are you talking about?" Dad asked.

"Dad," Matt said, "Chip's been bugging Charlie ever since he got here."

"That's no excuse—" Dad started.

"But it is, Daddy!" the Squid said. "It's a *real good* excuse. First Chip kicked the soccer ball against the garage and you blamed Charlie and then Chip wouldn't sleep on the mattress so he got to sleep on Charlie's bed and then he shot off the rocket when he wasn't supposed to and it almost hit Mrs. Walcott then he tried to hog all the rolls and ate the Swedish Fish and then he was jumping all around when Charlie was trying to watch his favorite show and he's really, really *a-n-o...*" She paused for a minute, trying to figure out how to spell something. Then she tried again. "Annoying: *a-n-o-i-e-e-i-n-g.*"

"Dad," Matt added, "he doesn't listen to any of us. Everybody always says what a great kid he is, but he's a pain."

"*P-a-i-n,*" spelled the Squid. "So I took the doorknob away. I was just trying to help Charlie."

Dad opened his mouth to say something but no words came out. He sat down on the bed and rubbed his head. A couple of minutes earlier, it had looked like he wanted to strangle all of us, but now I thought maybe I was going to live.

"Charlie?" he said.

"Yeah?"

"It sounds like you've had a hard time."

I nodded.

Dad took a deep breath. "Okay, look—"

Someone knocked on the door. Uncle Ron opened it and peeked in. "Everybody okay in here?"

"Yeah," Dad said. "Ron, could you see what you can do about that bathroom doorknob so it never comes off again?"

"Sure thing!" Uncle Ron said and shut the door again.

"Okay," Dad said. "It sounds like Chip can be a pain in the neck."

"A turkey butt," the Squid announced.

"But you don't get to lock him in the bathroom just because he bugs you. Whatever you think of Chip, he's got a new baby sister, and that can be hard."

That was true. I knew what baby sisters were like.

"Charlie, Chip is only here until tomorrow morning," Dad went on, "so you still have to put up with him and be as nice as you can to him. Even if he is *a-n-n-o-y-i-n-g*."

"Does that spell 'annoying'?" the Squid asked.

"Yes, it does, Squirt," Dad said. He got up from the bed, then reached out and messed up my hair.

"What if he says something dumb?" the Squid asked.

"Then bite your tongue," Dad said.

She scrunched up her face. "How does biting your tongue help?"

"It's just a saying," Dad told her. "It means sometimes it's better to keep your thoughts to yourself."

The Squid stuck out her tongue and bit on it. "Ow!" she said.

I was still thinking about all the things Chip had done. "Dad, he broke my Buck Meson Transport Module. And then he threw up in my bed."

"I know you worked hard on the model. All we can do now is get another one."

"What about a new bed?" Matt grinned. "Does Charlie have to sleep in barf from now on?"

"*B-A-R-F!*" the Squid spelled loudly.

"*B-A-R-P-H!*" Matt said.

"That's not right!" the Squid said.

"I know," Matt said.

"I'm sure your mom can take care of the bed situation, Charlie," Dad told me.

When we came out of their bedroom, Uncle Ron had just finished tightening the bathroom doorknob. We all started down the stairs. I was hoping I could see whatever was left of the Buck Meson special.

"Charlie?" a weak voice called from my room. It was Chip.

I went back and looked in. Mom had changed the sheets and Chip was in my bed under the covers.

"Hi, Chip. Are you okay?" I asked.

"I threw up on your bed," he said.

I nodded.

"Can you stay here?" he asked.

"I'll sit here with you for a while," Mom said.

"I want *Charlie* to stay," Chip said.

He looked pretty miserable. And I'd already missed most of the show anyway. "It's okay, Mom,"

I said. "I'll stay for a little while."

"All right." Mom got up and gave me a hug. "Call if you need anything," she said as she left the room.

"Could you sit here on the bed, Charlie?" Chip asked.

I sat down. The broken Buck Meson Transport Module was sitting on my nightstand.

"Was the show good?" Chip asked.

I shrugged. "I didn't get to see all of it."

"Just stay here until I go to sleep," he whispered. His eyelids were getting heavy.

"Okay." I picked up the broken model, wondering if we could glue it back together.

"I broke it," he mumbled.

"I know."

"And I pulled the rocket string too soon."

"Yeah," I said, staring at the pieces in my hands.

"And I threw up in your bed."

"I know."

"Charlie, I'm…"

It sounded like he wanted to say something that was hard to say. In a flash, I realized he was trying to say he was sorry. I waited a few seconds, then looked over at him. His mouth was open. His eyes were closed. The Perfect Little Turkey started to snore a little.

I heard the phone ring, then Matt called up the stairs. "Charlie, Tommy's on the phone."

I stood up and tiptoed out of the room. When I got to the kitchen, Matt handed me the phone.

"Hi, Tommy," I said.

"Hi. Guess what."

"What?"

"I didn't see it."

"Didn't see what?" I asked.

"Buck Meson, you bozo! I missed the TV special! We had a flat tire on the way home. We spent the whole time waiting for my uncle to come help us fix it. By the time we got here, it was over!"

"Guess what," I said. "I didn't see it either! I

guess we'll have to hope they show it again."

After I hung up, I turned around. Matt was leaning against the kitchen counter with a smug grin on his face.

"What's so funny?" I said.

"So Tommy didn't get to see it either."

"What's funny about that?"

"Did you forget what I said?"

"What?"

"Didn't I tell you I'd make sure you saw the Buck Meson show?"

"Yeah, but then Chip got locked in the bathroom and threw up. I only saw half of it."

"No problem. I set it up to record while you were taking Mrs. Walcott's Maserati to the car."

"You did?"

"Yeah. Now you and Tommy can watch that dumb show whenever you want."

"Thanks, Matt," I said.

"It's going to cost you," he said with his older brother smirk.

I didn't care. I went back in the family room to watch the show, but Mom and Dad came in and told me it was too late and I should go to bed.

I was okay with that. I was pretty tired. And it would be more fun to wait and watch it with Tommy anyway.

17

Whoops!

The next morning Uncle Brandon and Aunt Sarah and Pops and Gams came over for breakfast. Dad made pancakes. Uncle Ron decided we needed to have bacon, which we never get to have, so he went out and bought some. He made a big mess when he cooked it in the frying pan, but it tasted great. Chip ate about five slices. You'd never know that he'd been sick the night before.

When Aunt Sarah and Uncle Brandon heard how Chip had gotten locked in the bathroom (by accident) and had thrown up, they told him what a big brave boy he was. He smiled and nodded and ate another piece of bacon.

I looked at Matt. He rolled his eyes.

The Squid stuck her tongue out and bit down on it with her teeth.

Finally it was time for them to go. We all stood in the driveway giving hugs and saying good-bye. Aunt Sarah leaned over to me. "Charlie, thanks for having Chip stay with you. He told me he'd love to come see you again."

"Okay," I said. Then I bit my tongue, too. Ouch.

"Good-bye, Charlie!" Chip waved out of his window.

"Good-bye, Chip," I called back.

We all waved as they drove away.

"Phew," Dad said.

"You can say that again," Matt said.

"I'm so glad everyone came," Mom said. "It was a lot of people in our house, but it was worth it. Thanks, guys."

"And girl," said the Squid.

The soccer ball was sitting in the yard. I ran over and started dribbling it. Mom, Dad, Mabel, and Matt went inside.

"Hey, Charlie!" Uncle Ron yelled. "Pass it over here."

We kicked it back and forth. Uncle Ron had told me how much he loved playing soccer when he was a kid.

"How hard can you kick it, Uncle Ron?"

"They used to call me Bigfoot," he said. "Watch this."

He dribbled the ball over onto the driveway in front of the garage, then trapped it. "Bigfoot Bumpers on a break!" he shouted in his announcer's voice. "He's all alone. He sees an opening!"

"Uncle Ron, no! We're not supposed to—"
BAM!

He kicked it really hard. Harder than I'd ever kicked it. The ball flew up through the air like a rocket.

CRASH!

It broke through one of the little windows on the garage door.

"Whoops," Uncle Ron said.

My dad came out on the porch. "Charlie! Are you crazy? For the millionth time—"

"Hold it, bro," Uncle Ron said. "*He* didn't do it. *I* did. Sorry."

My dad shook his head and rubbed his eyes.

"But no harm," Uncle Ron said. "Charlie's going to help me fix it. We'll go the hardware store right now for the glass."

Without waiting for Dad to say anything, Uncle Ron headed to his truck. "Come on, Charlie," he said.

"Be back in time for lunch, you turkeys!" Dad yelled.

"No problem," Uncle Ron answered. "We never miss a meal."

We climbed in the truck and put on our seat belts. Uncle Ron looked over at me. "This will give us just enough time to shoot off rocket number two," he said. "I built it last night. It's in the back of the truck, already filled up with water."

"Stupific!" I said.

"Stupific," he agreed. "Whatever that means."

I liked riding in Uncle Ron's pickup—I got to sit in the front, since there were no backseats.

Uncle Ron was whistling to himself and started slapping the steering wheel in time.

I looked out the side window. From way up here in the truck, things looked different.

I thought about everything that happened yesterday. About Ginger not eating the brussels sprouts and the rocket flying sideways into the house and Grandma's yeast rolls and Buck Meson and Team Bumpers.

And Chip, the Perfect Little Turkey.

I wondered if Matt and the Squid and I would laugh about all those things when we grew up, like Dad and Uncle Ron laughed about the whipped cream, or Mom and Aunt Sarah laughed about green hair. Maybe someday I would even laugh about the broken transport module and Chip would laugh about throwing up the Swedish Fish.

And then, I thought of Mrs. Burke again. And my assignment. Right then, I knew what my definition of family was going to be.

"Uncle Ron," I said, "do you know what I think a family is?"

"What, Charlie?"

"People who love you and accept you, even when you're a bozon."

"Are you talking about me?" he asked with a grin.

"Yeah. And me, too. And Matt. And Mabel. And everyone."

"Everyone in this family is a bozon?"

"I think so," I said. "At least some of the time."

He laughed. "Works for me."

It worked for me, too.

Don't miss the other books
in the Charlie Bumpers series—
Charlie Bumpers vs. the Teacher of the Year,
Charlie Bumpers vs. the Really Nice Gnome,
Charlie Bumpers vs. the Squeaking Skull, and
Charlie Bumpers vs. the Puny Pirates.

Also available as audio books.

HC: 978-1-56145-732-8
PB: 978-1-56145-824-0
CD: 978-1-56145-770-0

HC: 978-1-56145-740-3
PB: 978-1-56145-831-8
CD: 978-1-56145-788-5

HC: 978-1-56145-808-0
PB: 978-1-56145-888-2
CD: 978-1-56145-809-7

HC: 978-1-56145-939-1
CD: 978-1-56145-941-4

And watch for the sixth book
in the series, coming up soon!

BILL HARLEY is the author of the award-winning middle reader novels *The Amazing Flight of Darius Frobisher* and *Night of the Spadefoot Toads*. He is also a storyteller, musician, and writer who has been writing and performing for kids and families for more than twenty years. Harley is the recipient of Parents' Choice and ALA awards, as well as two Grammy Awards. He lives in Massachusetts.

www.billharley.com

ADAM GUSTAVSON has illustrated many books for children, including *Lost and Found; The Blue House Dog; Mind Your Manners, Alice Roosevelt!;* and *Snow Day!* He lives in New Jersey.

www.adamgustavson.com